UNDERCOVER INMATES

MADISON JOHNS

UNDERCOVER INMATES

http://madisonjohns.com

Sign up for Madison's mystery newsletter for a new release alerts and a chance to get them at a discounted price http://eepurl.com/4kFsH

From the Author...

There is only one prison in Michigan for women, Women's Huron Valley Corrections Facility, and I chose to use a fictitious Westbrook Prison.

Acknowledgments

Thanks to who will remain nameless for helping me portray prison life.

Undercover Inmates

Agnes Barton and Eleanor Mason's most riveting case yet!

For years Agnes and Eleanor longed to be taken seriously by law enforcement for their investigative skills, and when they're deputized to enter Westbrook Prison as undercover inmates they finally have their chance.

Westbrook's beautician, Trudy Taylor, was found dead during lockup and the inmates have threatened to riot after Warden Geyer's investigation of the incident falls short.

Agnes and Eleanor enter the prison without the inmates or prison staff knowing what they're there to do. With the encouragement of the inmates, Agnes and Eleanor make a bargain that the warden can't turn down — not if she wants to prevent a riot.

The investigators are in the worst place possible, struggling to integrate into the inmate population. As the investigation moves forward, the truth might be more than they can handle.

UNDERCOVER INMATES

Chapter One

Eleanor and I stumbled off the transport bus to line up near a corrections officer. I tried not to twist my wrist lest the handcuffs chafe my wrists more than they already had. I swallowed hard as the Westbrook Prison loomed ahead. Would Eleanor and I be able to pull this off? Could we really mingle among the inmates undetected — as undercover inmates?

My husband Andrew wouldn't be happy about this, but he was in Detroit on a case, and he'd taken Eleanor's Mr. Wilson along, I think for comedic relief. This might be our most dangerous case yet. We were deputized, but we'd have to hold our own, which meant no help from either the warden or the corrections officers. Even they didn't know why we were here. Our job was simple: find out who killed the prison beautician before the inmates rioted. Apparently these women take losing a prison beautician hard. She was an inmate, but that doesn't mean she's any less important. That's why Eleanor and I took on this case.

From here on out, I wouldn't be Agnes Barton private investigator. I had a prison number or was simply called Barton. Eleanor was Mason.

"Hurry up, Barton," Officer Miller said sweetly.

"One of these days you'll have to toughen up, Miller, or you'll have the inmates walking all over you," Officer Barlow said. "I'm Officer Barlow and this is Officer Miller. She'll be taking you inside. Follow our orders and we won't have a problem."

Miller frowned for a moment and quickly went back to being stone-faced. From what I've seen so far, that's the expression all the officers wear. That's understandable. Their job isn't easy, but I'm curious about how it is from the inmates' point of views.

Miller motioned us forward with her baton, and we walked inside and along a corridor until she stopped and said, “That’s far enough. Keep along the wall to the right until your name is called. You’ll then proceed into that office.”

I waited as Eleanor’s last name was called first. When she emerged from the room, she said, “It’s the standard strip search and handing over of valuables -- including my wedding ring!”

“That’s enough, Mason,” Miller said. “They’ll find out when it’s their turn.”

After processing, we each held an orange shirt and pants; a small bag containing toothpaste, toothbrush; and shampoo in the tiniest bottle I’ve ever seen. I was shocked to discover the large room we were led into contained eight beds.

“We have to share a cell with eight women?” I asked.

“You’re not in a pod yet,” Miller informed me. “This is quarantine.”

“What does that mean?” Eleanor asked.

“You’ll be here until we know you don’t have anything contagious.”

When Officer Barlow entered the room, Miller

barked, “Get dressed and we’ll take you the commissary where you can purchase supplies, unless you like the standard toothpaste and shampoo. It will be hardly enough to last you long.”

“How can we go there if you think we might be contagious?” I asked.

“You know, you’re right.”

The sighs of the other inmates gave me pause. I had inconvenienced us all. I chalked that up to a newbie mistake. I only hoped the other inmates would feel that way, too, and cut me some slack.

As Eleanor and I changed into our orange prison uniforms the first thing that came to my mind was how much I missed my privacy. Well, that and my freedom and my Andrew. I wasn’t sure I was ready for this culture shock.

I sat across from a thin blonde who couldn’t weigh ninety pounds wet. Tears rolled down her face before they fell to her palms where they pooled.

“Hello there,” I greeted her. “My name is Agnes

Barton and this is Eleanor Mason."

"H-Hi," is all she could manage.

"I hope I don't have to hear her sniveling all night," a portly woman griped.

"Leave her alone, Jessy," a tall, thin woman said. "I'm Mel." She fluffed her gray hair. "Believe it or not, I'm not even forty yet. Premature gray hair is what I got going on." She laughed.

"I-I'm Laura," the crying woman finally eked out.

"Is this when we're supposed to ... you know tell each other why we're in here?" Eleanor asked.

Laura glanced up and then back at her lap. "I'd rather forget," she said.

"I'd kill the crying stuff before we head to the pod," Jessy said. "It's better to hold your own in here."

Jessy spoke to Laura in a gruff voice, but I imagined her advice was stellar. I kept trying to remember my story about why I'm in prison just in case anyone asks.

Office Miller returned. "I'll take your

commissary orders now, providing you have money in your accounts."

"I-I don't," Laura said.

"Don't worry, I'll order what you need." I whispered to Laura, as Mel, Jezzy and Eleanor blocked Laura from Officer Miller. "I'll order extra shampoo, conditioner, toothpaste and deodorant."

"Oh no, I couldn't allow you to do that. I don't know when or how I'll be able to pay you back."

How? What did she mean by that?

I didn't have to ponder long when Laura informed me, "I'm not like that, you know. I have a boyfriend -- or I used to."

I nodded. "I don't have to guess why you're in here then. I imagine that boyfriend you had helped put you here. I have a husband."

I approached Miller. "I'd like to order two of the deodorant, shampoo, conditioner, and soup. I mean soap." When the officer gave me an odd look, I added. "Also double toothpaste and toothbrushes."

"Are you sure you want to spend your account

money on toiletries for another inmate?"

"I have no idea what you mean."

She nodded toward Laura. "Since she's the only one not hightailing it up here, you must be buying her toiletries."

"No," I lied. "I just go through toiletries like there's no tomorrow."

"Hmm," Miller buzzed as I moved to where Eleanor waited with Mel and Jessy.

Jessy shook her head at me as the new inmate approached and introduced herself as Char. "I couldn't help but notice that you ordered for two. Is there something we need to know about?"

"I use a lot of shampoo and conditioner. I mean, I really didn't know how much to order."

Char rolled her eyes and put one hand on my shoulder to get my attention before letting it drop to her side. "Look, you remind me of my grandmother so I'll give you some advice. You've been played." She pointed to Laura. "That sweet thing over there is no more in need than you. She knows how to turn those doe-like eyes on whenever she wants something. She has an account like the rest of us."

My hands slipped to my hips. "And how can you be so sure?"

"We were in the Oakland County jail together. She's been playing the, 'Oh, I don't have any money in my account business' since she's been locked up."

My lips formed an O. "I see. Well, I'm still not sorry for trying to help her out. I don't need any bad karma coming my way."

Char laughed. "I believe we've all been shown just how bad karma can get or none of us would be here, now, would we?"

I nodded. "You know you're right."

"She doesn't mean to be a know-it-all," Eleanor said. "Agnes can't seem to help herself."

Char narrowed her eyes and glared at Eleanor. I said, "This is Eleanor. She's a good friend."

"So what are you two in here for?" Jessy asked with a blank stare.

"Armed robbery," I said while at the same time

Eleanor exclaimed, “Grand theft auto.”

“So which is it?” Jessy asked with a near sneer.

“I robbed a bank,” I insisted.

“And I stole a car and was the getaway driver,” Eleanor added. “It seemed like a good idea up until the time I slammed into a cop car when Agnes came out with the loot.”

Char laughed. “Thanks for the image. It’s hard to find things to laugh about in this place.”

“You’ve obviously been in prison before” I said.

“It’s been a revolving door for me, I’m afraid,” Char said. “I really thought I’d be out for the long haul, but I just don’t do good on the outside.”

“She’s in for attempted murder,” Jessy said with a smile.

“I should have known that good-for-nothing husband was up to no good when he didn’t pick me up from prison. So, I might have thrown a few punches when I caught him with that bartender.”

“Would that be a few dozen?” Mel asked.

“So what are you in for Mel?” Char asked.

Mel shrugged. “Embezzlement. When I wasn’t

caught the first time, I didn't think I ever would be. I guess I was wrong."

"Sounds like all you women are in here for a long haul," Jessy said. "I'm only here for probation violation. Have to serve the last six months of my original sentence for uttering and publishing."

"Bad checks?" Eleanor replied. "And here I thought you were in for murder."

Jessy's face twisted into a snarl and she took a step toward Eleanor. "Why would you think that?"

"It must be you sunny disposition." Char laughed.

"So nobody is here for murder," I mused aloud. "I suppose that's a good thing since there are way too many murders according to those crime shows on television."

"You watch crime shows?" Jessy asked.

"How else are we going to figure out how to not get caught," Eleanor said. "I must have missed the one on how not to get caught when you're the getaway driver." She sighed. "I wish I had just borrowed my mother's car."

Jessy locked eyes with Eleanor and asked, "Is your mother still alive ?"

"Mind your business," Char said. "Show some respect."

"Just because you're a frequent flier doesn't mean what you say goes."

"Try me and see," Char threatened with a raise of her chin.

Jessy didn't rise to the challenge, instead remaining seated on her bunk until Char walked to the far side of the room. That's when Jessy jumped up and bumped her shoulder into mine. "Char won't always be around you know."

I suppose I should have felt intimidated, but Jessy only riled me. Her tough act wasn't cutting t with me. I only hoped I wouldn't be pushed into an altercation with her.

"You better watch it with her," Eleanor whispered as Jessy walked away.

"It's fine. I have it handled."

"This isn't a women's prison show, Agnes. You could really get hurt if that Jessy gets irritated with you."

"I'm not worried about it. Besides, what are the odds she'll be put in the same pod as us?"

Laura sat quietly on her bed, not engaging with anyone. Eleanor and I sat on either side of her on her bunk. "Are you always a quiet one?" I asked.

"It's better that way."

"What are you in for?"

She shrugged.

"What's the big secret? Did you murder someone?" Eleanor pressed.

Laura gazed up at us. "Please leave me alone."

"Fine, but it's going to lonely in here if you never speak to anyone," I replied as we left.

"Maybe she's right. It might be better for us to keep a low profile, too," Eleanor suggested.

"Except that we'll have to interact with the prisoners if we're to find out who killed the beautician. I only hope we'll get out of quarantine soon."

Chapter Two

"Barton, the nurse will see you now," the gruff officer said. She stood six feet, two inches tall, with the build of a linebacker.

I gave her nametag a quick look. "Right away, Officer Schulze."

"Can I go with her?" Eleanor asked.

"What is it with you two? Are you girlfriends?" She laughed. Her smile quickly faded. "Sit back down, Mason."

Eleanor begrudgingly did as she was told, but with a sneer on her face. "How do you know anything about us? This is the first time you've seen us," Eleanor muttered to herself.

"If you have something to say to me, Mason, speak up."

Eleanor clammed up, which made me happy

because I didn't want to see her written up.

"That's what I thought. In case you're wondering, Barlow gave me the rundown about all you newbies." Schulze stared at Char for a moment before adding, "And you frequent fliers."

I walked into the other room and greeted the nurse as I sat in the blood collection chair, offering her my right arm. "I have deep veins," I informed her. She wrapped the rubber band above my elbow and I suffered as she tapped my arm and dug deep to find a usable vein. "Did I mention that I hate needles?"

"Nobody cares."

I remained silent after that. Although the nurse was pleasant enough, I wondered how long it would be before the quarantine was completed. We had been here more than two weeks now whiling away our time. We certainly would not be able to solve any case while stuck in quarantine.

"Send Mason in," the nurse said, looking at a stack of forms.

I walked into the other room and tagged

Eleanor for her turn.

Then it was time to meet the doctor. I smiled as I sat in the exam room. The doctor's dark curls swayed as she listened to my heart with the frosty stethoscope. She was younger than I imagined.

"I'm Doctor Wright," she said.

"At least you're not the wrong doctor," I joked.

She smiled for a fraction of a second. "Do you have any health problems I should be aware of?"

"I have a nagging hip and my right knee has been bothering me."

"I'll make a note of that for the warden. It might help with your job assignments."

"Thanks, I'd appreciate that."

The remainder of the day consisted of waiting in the quarantine cell, staring at the walls or the bottoms of the upper bunks.

Schulze opened the cell door and tapped her clipboard. "It looks like it's time for you ladies to learn what real prison life is all about," she said. "Gather your belongings and follow me to the linen room. I expect all of you are strong enough to lug your mattress and linen to your cells. You're all in F Pod."

Char gasped. "You can't send Agnes and Eleanor there. They'll be eaten alive."

"Do you want to spend your first night back in solitary, Char?"

Char kept silent after that. "What's wrong with that pod?" I asked in a whisper.

"It's a step down from maximum security, but many of the inmates are not right in the head. Keep to yourselves."

* * *

As Eleanor and I entered the pod I tried not to make eye contact with anyone.

Inmates congregated in the center of the large room, catcalling, which I believe was meant to intimidate the new inmates. Of course, Eleanor didn't seem to mind, playing along with a bob of her head in greeting. I didn't pay all the much attention as I struggled to carry what the prison considered a mattress and bedding. At least it smelled clean.

I stared at the open cells on two different levels connected by metal stairs. “Barton and Mason, this is your cell. You have five minutes to get you bunks in order,” Officer Schulze barked.

I was relieved to find that the cell we walked into had only two beds — and that Eleanor and I were together. “This is certainly close quarters,” I said.

“Shh, we only have five minutes, remember?” Eleanor said.

We hurried to make our beds, and Officer Schulze introduced us to Maria Lopez. “She’s a trustee. If you have any questions, direct them to her.”

“Right this way, ladies,” Lopez said. “I’ll give you a tour of the facilities.”

We walked into the shower room. The stalls were tiny, but at least they had curtains offering some privacy. Lopez then took us down a long hallway, where Eleanor stopped at a large sign over a closed door. It read Beautician.

“So there is a hair salon. Great,” Eleanor

exclaimed with a sigh. "I really am in need of a cut and style."

"We have a salon, but are short a beautician. The last one was found dead in the shower room. She was found after lockup, so a few of the inmates are talking riot if the warden doesn't find the killer soon," Lopez whispered.

"Do they think an officer was involved?" I asked.

"That's the consensus. How else would she be out of her cell during lockup? It smells wrong, if you ask me."

"What was her name?" I asked.

"I wouldn't start asking too many questions if I were you."

"Trudy Taylor," Char offered. "My sister is locked up here, too. Or was until she was paroled last week. Our mother relayed the information to me when I found out I was coming to Westbrook."

"I didn't mean to pry. I have an interest in solving mysteries."

"That's a good pastime I suppose, but I'm not

sure how the other inmates might feel about it," Lopez commented.

Lopez led us into a room housing tables with benches bolted to the floor, past metal steam tables lining the front of the area.

"This is the chow hall," Lopez explained. "The first thing that's hard to get used to is being constantly supervised. Cameras are positioned in most areas, but I'm sure you'll find out where the blind spots are in time. Stay away from them, no matter what anyone tells you."

She led us back to the pod's open area, and when we sat down inquisitive inmates surrounded us. "So what you in for, Blondie?" they first asked Laura.

She glanced down until a brawny inmate pounded her fist on the table, causing Eleanor and me to jump.

Laura then looked up angrily. "Murder. I'm a psycho killer; how's that?" She stood up and clenched her hands into fists. "If anyone hassles me, they'll be sorry. I might be small, but I have one hell of a punch."

Laura walked back to her cell as the inmates laughed and hooted after her. "It was easy to break her," an inmate said. "She's no more a murderer than I'm a nun."

I remained silent, thumbing through a tattered magazine until Char said, "Time to line up for chow."

Eleanor and I followed the inmates into the chow hall, but I became concerned when I didn't see Laura join the line.

"Let's head back and find Laura," I whispered to Eleanor.

"But we haven't even gotten our food yet. I'm hungry."

"Would you rather eat and allow poor Laura to be harmed? You heard how she talked to the other inmates. That spells sure trouble for her."

Eleanor reluctantly followed me down the hallway when Schulze stopped us. "Where do you think you're going?" she asked. "Chow's the other direction."

"We have to use the bathroom."

"Hurry it up," she said as she led us to the bathroom and posted herself outside the door.

"How are we going to get out of here without that Amazon following us?" Eleanor asked once we were inside the bathroom.

"You could keep her busy while I look for Laura."

"Do you think that's wise?"

"Probably not, but what else can we do?"

We waited a few minutes before Eleanor walked from the bathroom. "Agnes might be a while," Eleanor told Schulze. "I'm hungry."

"I guess you'll be eating scraps tonight then because I'm not moving."

I crept out of the bathroom as Eleanor and Schulze continued their debate. I hurried around the corner that led back to the pod. I ignored the cameras as I made a sweep of the cells, listening for any sounds that carried because of the echo effect.

Thump...

I moved in the direction of the showers and

crept inside and found Laura smoking a cigarette with the same inmate who had challenged her earlier. I hurried back out of the room at the sound of footsteps moving in my direction. I raced back to where Eleanor and Schulze had been, but because they were gone I walked back to the chow hall alone. I had stood in line no more than a minute when Schulze walked over to me, her nostrils flaring slightly.

"How did you slip past me at the shower?"

"I don't know. I walked right past you while you and Eleanor were talking. Perhaps you need glasses or a hearing aid."

"Maybe you'd like a night in solitary."

"Leave her alone, Schulze," said a woman dressed in a skirt and matching jacket, and heels. I suspected she was the warden, although I didn't recall that Westbrook had a female warden. A younger man dressed in suit and tie flanked her.

"But she was AWOL."

"I'm aware of where she was at all times. Kindly release Mason from solitary. I don't need our newcomers to be deprived of dinner on their first night in the pod."

I didn't know which shocked me more, that this woman censured the officer in front of the inmates or that Eleanor had been sent to solitary for what I had done.

"I'm Warden Geyer and this is the Deputy Director Smith," the woman explained.

"Hello, Barton. You had us worried for a moment, but I can see the situation has been rectified. Consider that your one and only warning. You had better find a way to make peace with Schulze or your stay will be a long one," Deputy Director Smith said.

"Thank you. I really didn't mean to break any rules."

"Did you find what you were looking for?" Warden Geyer asked.

"No. I thought someone was missing, but I can see she's sitting right over there," I said, not indicating who I meant. I didn't want to break any inmate codes of conduct.

Eleanor huffed and puffed as she joined me in the chow line. I didn't even notice what was thrown on my tray until we found a seat. Yuck! Beef over noodles that tasted like mush, the beef too hard to chew with my dentures.

I swallowed it down with black coffee that tasted nothing like my vanilla creamer-enhanced coffee I drank back at home. I didn't think about how many sacrifices I'd have to make.

I yawned by the time dinner was over and shuffled into the main room.

"Stand in that line over there," Char said. "They hand out the nightly medications there."

I nodded, and Eleanor and I fidgeted as we took turns checking the length of the line.

After we had taken our medications - an act observed by a corrections officer — I followed Eleanor back to our cell instead of congregating in the rec room with most of the inmates. Fortunately we weren't bothered, and I dozed off until the doors of the cell slammed closed.

It was hard not to cringe at the sound of the

other inmates moving in their cells. And a solid night's sleep was impossible with the officers walking past with their flashlights trained on us.

I couldn't imagine what it would be like to live like this for years and years. It was hardly living at all.

It appeared we would survive our first night in our pod. After nearly three weeks in prison all we had learned was the name of the beautician.

Chapter Three

I covered my eyes as the blast of lights came on in the morning. It's the only way I could discern where I was, and it came crashing down on me that I wasn't home in bed, but in a cramped cell in Westbrook Prison.

Today would be our first full day in the regular population, and I hoped to make the most of it investigation-wise.

We hurried to make our bunks before an officer showed up to give us grief. We then followed the other prisoners into the chow hall.

I stood in line behind Eleanor until it was our turn at the steam table, where oatmeal and scrambled eggs were plopped on our plates. I nodded kindly to the woman working the steam table. A woman who was about our age motioned us over to a table near the door.

"Can we sit here?" I asked.

The large woman smiled slightly, wrinkles creasing her face. "Why else did you think I called you over here?"

I shrugged and sat down. "Thank you."

"No need to thank anyone, but you should have been given a hash brown patty. I was planning to ask if you'd like to trade me the hash brown for a my piece of bacon."

My mouth watered. "That sounds like a good trade. I'll go right back up there to ask for one," I said.

I marched back up to the chow line and indeed saw the aforementioned hash brown that I hadn't been given. "Could I please have the hash brown?" I asked politely. "You must have forgotten to give it to me."

"Is that right?" the woman asked with a chuckle. "I guess you'll have to try back tomorrow. I don't feel like giving you a hash brown today."

My brow shot up. "And why not?" I demanded.

"I could be convinced if you could give me your pin number. I need to call my mother." She grinned.

"I imagine you might, but I forgot my pin number. At my age I barely remember my name."

"It looks like we might have a problem then, because I'm not giving you anything without you paying me."

"I imagine you'd feel that way, but I'm not about to barter with you. I'm already bartering with someone else."

"Stop it, Teresa," the woman next to her said. "Don't let her scare you. I'm Jana." She put a hash brown on a plate and handed it to me.

"Thank you, Jana. I'm sorry if I've overstepped, Teresa. I'm figuring out how things work here."

I sat down and presented the hash brown to the woman in exchange for a piece of cold bacon, which I devoured without complaining. I had achieved a victory. I conducted my first prison trade.

A voice came over the intercom: "Report to

Hallway A to receive your work assignments after breakfast."

"Where is Hallway A, I wonder," I said.

"It's very confusing with all the twist and turns of this place," Eleanor admitted.

I smiled hopefully at the woman across from me, but from her frowning face, I assumed she'd be of no help.

"I wonder when we can take a shower," I said.

The woman crossed her arms and said, "You should have done that before you came to breakfast. Some inmates even shower instead of breakfast." She pushed up from the table, depositing the hash brown into her pocket.

Char met us outside the chow hall and smiled. "I thought you wouldn't mind horribly if I showed you the ropes. Hallway A is this way. I saw what happened when you disappeared on Schulze. I'm sure you're aware that wasn't the smartest move. She can be a tyrant at times, but she's certainly an officer to have in your corner."

I nodded, although I couldn't imagine Schulze

to be anything but difficult. Perhaps it was time to listen to the wisdom of others. I really was glad that Char was helping us out, even if I wasn't sure her kindness would last all that long – or whether it had a price. We could hardly expect her to take us under her wing, especially when we had our own agenda.

Eleanor and I stood in the back of the line as names were called and inmates moved along to their assignments.

"I wonder what jobs we'll be given. I hope we can remain together," I said to Eleanor.

"Barton and Mason, I'll take you to the offices," Officer Barlow said. "You'll be cleaning them today."

Eleanor and I smiled, happy with our assignments. Not because cleaning the offices would be easy compared to some assignments, but because we might be able to gather useful information while we were there. That was my hope, anyway.

"How do you just come in here and get a cushy

job like that," an inmate complained.

"Now, Velma, I remember when you first came here," another inmate said. "You were under the weather and didn't have a work assignment for an entire week."

Velma smiled. "You're right, Yolanda. Thankfully nobody gave me any grief about it. But you noticed how the warden treated them at dinner in the chow room."

Yolanda locked eyes with me. "That was only an act because the deputy director was here, and you know it. When was the last time you've seen the warden showing off her pretty legs in our chow hall? I'll tell you when—never!"

"I can't believe that an investigation isn't ongoing to find out who killed the beautician," I said.

Velma's eyes blazed. "Who told you about that?"

"I'd rather not reveal my source. I'm no snitch," I exclaimed.

"Fine, but you'll need to hear the whole story."

"We'll talk at lunch," Yolanda said with a nod. "I sure hope we find another beautician, and soon. I need a permanent in the worse way."

"Yolanda means she wants her hair straightened," Eleanor said. "Not curly."

"I'm perfectly aware of what she meant, Eleanor."

Eleanor and I followed Barlow to the offices. Her keys clanged together as she unlocked multiple doors. We made our way into a cleaning supply room, where another officer was positioned. "You'll have to check out your cleaning supplies with Officer Yates," Barlow explained.

"That will be one vacuum, mop bucket and cleaner tablet, window cleaner, spray bottle and dust cloth," Yates checked off her list.

"What? No broom and dustpan?" I asked with a smile.

"That's a given," Yates said.

Eleanor filled the mop bucket with the soap tablet and moved the cleaning cart from the room and up the hallway. I pushed the vacuum cleaner.

Barlow led us into the warden's office. "The warden is out today, but you can do a once over while I watch."

"Do you have to?" I asked. "I hate to be watched while I work."

"You had better get used to it."

I grumbled as I plugged in the vacuum while Eleanor emptied the wastebaskets. Was it too much to hope that we'd find a document in one?

We moved from the warden's office to the psychiatrist's office, where a rather good-looking man was seated behind a desk. "Hello, you must be new here."

"Does it show?" I asked.

"I'm Dr. Franks. I expect I'll be seeing the both of you soon. I would have earlier, but I was out of the office for a conference and only returned today."

I merely nodded as Barlow stood a few feet from us. I didn't want to get into any trouble.

"Officer Barlow, why don't you busy yourself elsewhere? I'd like to speak with the women alone."

"But they're assigned to work now. You'll have to schedule appointments at a later time."

Dr. Franks stood. "I imagine the warden wouldn't mind. Should I ask her?"

"She's not in the prison—" Barlow sighed. "Very well, but don't keep them long."

I relaxed slightly when the door closed behind the officer. "It's nice to meet you, doctor. I'm Agnes Barton."

"And I'm Eleanor Mason."

"It's nice to meet you ladies. I believe I have you on my schedule in a few days. How are things going so far?"

"Just fine for prison, I suppose," I said.

"It's quite an adjustment," Eleanor added. "But at least we're roomed together."

Dr. Franks moved to his computer, clacking the keys as he typed. Then he frowned. "It's highly unlikely that you two should even be in the same prison or pod since you committed your crimes together."

"Please don't separate us," I pleaded. "I swear, all we want is to serve our time with as few problems as possible."

"I understand that we're in prison and here to serve our time. I didn't expect to be given privileges," Eleanor said. "But we need each other to adjust to life here. We have no plans to violate prison rules."

Dr. Franks looked up at us. "I suppose you're right. Obviously there was a reason you've been allowed to stay together. At least this way you'll be less of a target for physical abuse after lockup."

"Are you certain," I said. "I heard the beautician was murdered during lockup."

"Have the prisoners mentioned what they have planned to do?"

"They need a new beautician, if that's what you mean."

"That's exactly what I meant, but if you catch wind of anything in regard to the inmates planning to take matters into their own hands, please let me know. I'd hate for anyone else to be hurt."

"I'm sure a new beautician is all they need," I suggested.

"Will we be able to clean your office now?" Eleanor asked.

"Sure. I need to step out for a few moments anyway."

We waited until the doctor left and were surprised when Officer Barlow didn't mosey into the office. We did what we came to do: search his office.

"Hurry up, Eleanor," I whispered.

Eleanor glanced up in the corner. "Let's just do our regular cleaning. I believe our movements are being tracked," she said, nodding toward the security camera.

"Got ya. I suppose it's too much to hope that an incriminating file would be open for us to glance at while we clean."

I vacuumed and hummed while Eleanor wiped down the desk, which would be the perfect opportunity to upset a file enough that it would fall to the floor. Of course she didn't do that since she believed we were being watched.

With the wastebasket dumped into the larger trash bag on the cart, and the vacuum pushed further down the hallway, Lopez approached us.

"I'm supposed to be supervising you now. Officer Barlow had to leave for a meeting."

"Oh? I was under the impression that we'd be watched by her the whole time we were cleaning today."

"I'm sure she told you that, but she seldom follows through."

"Except when we cleaned the warden's office," I said.

"The employee bathrooms are part of your job, too." She smiled. "I'll be waiting in the warden's lounge. It's right across the hall from her office. Knock before you enter."

I led the way into the bathroom, disgusted at the mess. You'd think the office bathrooms would be tidier.

"We had better slap on the rubber gloves for this," I volunteered.

Eleanor pulled gloves off the cart and we donned them. I swept the stalls and said, “It’s strange about Officer Barlow’s last-minute meeting don’t you think?”

“Yes, very. I rather like Lopez supervising us, though. Especially when she’s doing it from a lounge.” Eleanor laughed, filling the tissue dispensers.

I cleaned the mirrors and sinks. “All we need now is a good mop.”

“I know. You’d think that this prison would buy better mops heads.”

“I meant it’s time for you to mop, Eleanor.”

“Why me? What’s wrong with you?”

“I just swept, and cleaned the sinks and mirrors.”

“Well, I filled the tissue and emptied the trash.”

“Fine, I’ll mop if that makes you happy, Eleanor.”

“Well, one of us better hurry before someone comes looking for us.” Eleanor took hold of the mop, but didn’t do the best job. She was right; the mop was cheap and hardly big enough to do the job quickly.

Back in the hallway, I admitted, "I'm exhausted already."

"Me, too. I wonder what time lunch is."

We walked into another office, where a clock on the wall read ten o'clock. "Is that all it is?" I griped. "I would have thought it was much later."

"Perhaps we should meet up with Lopez. I bet she can tell us what time lunch is," Eleanor said.

We pushed the cart and vacuum cleaner back into the supply room. It wasn't lost on me that Officer Yates wasn't there. I rubbed my back as we moved up the hallway. Directly across from the warden's office was a door. I knocked and then turned the doorknob, but it wouldn't budge. I pressed an ear to the door. "Lopez," I called. "It's Agnes and Eleanor."

There was no response. Eleanor said, "Maybe she's not here now. She might have been caught not looking after us properly, or she was needed elsewhere."

"That works for me, but how will we find out what time lunch is. I suppose we'll have to do more cleaning until someone comes for us."

Eleanor sighed. "You're right. It's too bad though. Can't we find somewhere to slack off?"

I laughed as I retrieved the cleaning cart and pushed it up the hallway. "I hardly think that we should do that on our first day of our work detail."

"But they shouldn't expect us to do that, Agnes. We're both too old to keep up with cleaning. If this is a cushy job, I'd hate to see what hard labor is like."

We moved to the next office. "It seems unusually quiet for this early in the day," Eleanor commented.

"That's my thought, too. Where is everyone?"

"Lopez mentioned a meeting."

"But where would the meeting be if not in one of the offices?" I asked. "We passed quite a few offices already and haven't seen anyone." My stomach growled. "Perhaps if we keep walking we'll find someone."

"Or check in with the office guarding the cleaning supplies," Eleanor suggested.

"You mean the one that was missing from the supply room the last time we were in there?"

"Maybe she returned," Eleanor suggested.

We moved to the supply room, but when we entered the room, Officer Yates was nowhere to be found. "I'm beginning to worry now, Eleanor. Where is the officer who's supposed to be stationed here?"

"I don't know what to do, but we can't even get back to our pod without the aid of an officer."

We took turns mopping the hallway until the clacking of heels approached us. Officer Barlow and Doctor Franks walked side by side, laughing at something I couldn't hear.

"It's about time," Eleanor said. "What time is lunch?"

Barlow glanced at her watch. "It's only ten. Lunch isn't until noon."

"Don't we at least get a morning break?" I asked with a hopeful look in my eyes.

"You're not at home, you know," Barlow snapped back.

"I know, but where were you? I thought you were supposed to be watching us."

Fire shot from Barlow's eyes. "Don't even presume to question me, Barton!"

"Maybe I should take them back to the pod. They both look like they could use a break," Dr. Franks said.

"Fine, but you know this will be on you if their work isn't completed today."

Franks laughed. "Okay, Barlow. Whatever you say."

We put the cleaning cart and vacuum cleaner in the supply room. "It needs to be locked, Barlow," I said, smiling when her eyes narrowed.

Chapter Four

The pod was empty except for Laura, who was sitting in the main room.

I decided for the moment to mind my own business. Ever since I saw her in the shower room, I couldn't help but wonder why she was really here. How was she able to become that chummy with another inmate so soon, and smoking a banned cigarette?

Eleanor and I relaxed in our cell, hoping it would remain quiet until lunch.

"Boo," said Char, standing at the entrance of our cell. "How did cleaning the office go?"

"Exhausting. Luckily they brought us back early for a break. It was more work than I thought it would be," I said.

"You'll get used to it. At least with a job you

don't get bored. Too much idle time spells trouble in here."

"Have you ever cleaned the offices?" I asked.

"No, why?"

"I just wondered."

"Let's head to the chow hall before the line gets too long," Eleanor suggested.

The line wasn't long at all, but long enough to warrant a ten-minute wait.

I smiled at Teresa, the woman who hadn't been very nice to me at breakfast. She slopped something long and white on my tray. "What is this supposed to be?"

"Lunch. Keep moving. You're holding up the line."

I didn't respond, and Jana winked at me while placing cornbread on my tray. That's all I wanted, although there were thin mashed potatoes — or I guessed that's what it was.

Eleanor and I sat by ourselves until the woman I had traded with at breakfast sat across from us.

"Hello again," she said eyeing my tray. "I didn't

get any cornbread."

I shrugged. "Perhaps you should go back up and ask for it."

The woman put her meaty paws on the table. "You can't ask for the cornbread. It has to be given to you." She smiled revealing a missing front tooth.

"I'm Agnes and this is Eleanor. I didn't get your name at breakfast."

"Chris, but they call me Crusher," she said as she clenched a fist.

I wasn't about to let that frighten me. And I wasn't all that happy that Crusher had decided to sit at our table. I had the sneaking suspicion that meant trouble for Eleanor and me.

"Nice to meet you, Crusher," Eleanor said. "I wasn't given any cornbread either. It must be a conspiracy."

Crusher stared me down. "Give me your cornbread."

"No. It's the only thing that looks appetizing. I don't even know what this white thing is."

"It's the warden's idea of fish," an inmate said

from across the aisle. "I have no idea if it's fish at all. I think it might be something else. All I know is I get the runs every time I eat it."

"It could be because of all the laxatives Dr. Wright gives you." Crusher said.

"But how else will I be able to lose weight?"

"You could quit buying so much from the commissary," Jessy said from across the table.

I tried not to react to Jessy. She was annoying enough in quarantine. I had already formed an opinion of her, and it wasn't good.

"Commissary? Isn't that only toiletry supplies?" I asked.

"Far from it," an inmate across from me said. "You can pick up things to make meals even." She smiled shyly, introducing herself as Carol.

"I had no idea. We didn't get the chance to go yet. We had to place our orders with an officer."

"You'd better stock up when you get there. You never know when our privileges might be taken away."

"They can take away commissary?" Eleanor

asked with widened eyes.

"Yes, and phone calls, even visits."

"That's awful," I said, catching Crusher's hand moving slowly to my tray. I yanked it back. "I said I'm not trading my cornbread with you."

"I'm not talking a trade." She slammed her fist on the table. "Give me that cornbread, now!"

Officer Schulze walked over. "What's the problem here?"

I shrugged and Crusher stood up and glared at me. "Nothing. Nothing at all!" She left, leaving me with the feeling that this wouldn't be the last I'd see of Crusher today. I wrapped the cornbread in a paper napkin and put it into my pocket. It might be a good snack for later. I was too keyed up to eat.

"Don't let her push you around," Carol said.

Jessy laughed. "Great job. You have angered the mighty Crusher. I'd sleep with one eye open if I were you."

I left the chow hall, not wishing to respond to Jessy's barb. I could hold my own — I'd have to.

I walked outside as yard time was announced.

Eleanor and I sat down and I pulled out my cornbread, breaking off a piece. But when I took a bite, I encountered plastic. I spit into my hand and found a small baggie containing two pills.

"Oh, no," Eleanor whispered. "No wonder Crusher wanted that cornbread."

"What should I do with it?"

"You don't want to get caught with it. Throw it in the trash."

I deposited the bag into the trash, cornbread and all. Before I could sit back down, two inmates dove into the trashcan.

"What are you doing over there?" Schulze asked the inmates.

They stood with their bodies against the trashcan. "Nothing. We wanted to make sure the trash bag didn't slip inside again. I'm on trash detail, and it's not fun to pick it out."

"It's gross," the second inmate said.

"Hello there, Agnes and Eleanor," Yolanda greeted us. "Me and Velma missed you at the chow hall. I thought you wanted to know about Trudy's death."

"We do," I said as we walked with them to the far side of the yard, where we sat on a bench. "So what happened?"

"Trudy was really a great lady. She's been doing hair at this prison for more than two years – until they found her body in the shower room that morning."

"How long ago did it happen?"

Yolanda wiped a tear away. "About a month ago."

"It had to be an officer," Velma insisted. "Nobody else would be out during lockup. Whoever took Trudy from her cell must have done it after the count."

"Did she have problems with any of the officers?"

"Sure. I mean she'd been to solitary when they caught her making hooch."

"What is hooch?" I asked.

"It's prison alcohol," Yolanda said. "It's hard to come by the ingredients, but when you know someone who works in the kitchen, it's doable."

"How was she caught?"

"During a cell shakedown. Strange thing is that it was happening more and more for Trudy. I suspect someone was trying to set her up."

"Someone snitched on her?" Eleanor asked.

"If they did, nobody found out about it," Velma said. "Snitches don't last long in here."

"Was Trudy the type to snitch on anyone else?"

"No, she'd never do that. She was too respected here."

"Getting back to the hooch," I said. "Was it something Trudy usually made?"

"We've all had a hand at it. I'm never shocked when any of us makes a batch," Yolanda said.

"So you weren't close to Trudy?"

"She did my hair, but that was the extent of it."

"Who was she close to?" I asked.

"It was one of the guards, I tell you," Velma said.

"I'd like to check every avenue. At least that's how I've always done it in the past."

"Agnes is good at solving mysteries."

"I'm glad to hear that. I'm not sure how long the inmates will keep their cool if the person who murdered Trudy isn't caught. I hope it is a guard and not one of us," Yolanda said.

"Who else was Trudy close too," I pressed.

"You didn't hear it from me," Yolanda said, looking around the yard, "but Kelly Nash was once her friend. She's in D Pod now. They were separated after they got too many 033s."

Eleanor looked puzzled.

"Sexual misconduct," Yolanda explained.

"So they were in a relationship?" Eleanor asked.

"Yes, a volatile one," Velma said. "I hardly think she could be involved with Trudy's murder. They moved her out of our pod before Trudy died."

"Are D Pod and F Pod ever in the yard at the same time?"

Yolanda nodded. "Once a week we have a volleyball game."

"You might want to question Fran Wilson,"

Velma said. “ And Trudy and Shelly Rhodes were mortal enemies.”

“That’s certainly turning out to be quite the list for someone who was so well respected.”

“Mary Phelps might be someone to ask, but she’s the prison drug dealer so you want to tread light with her,” Yolanda added.

“What about guards? Surely there had to be some she got along with — or didn’t,” I said.

“Not that she ever mentioned.”

“Had officers Schulze and Barlow been working the pod before Trudy was murdered?”

“Yes, but it will be hard to get a guard to talk. They stick together.”

“Just like us, I suppose,” I said. “Of course, they give Lopez leeway since she’s the trustee. She was supervising us when we were cleaning the offices.”

“What?” Yolanda said. “Under whose order?”

“Officer Barlow, I think. She was the one waiting outside the psychiatrist’s office after we cleaned it. I was surprised when Lopez was there to replace Barlow after the way she treated us, watching our every move."

"Barton and Mason, come with us," Officer Barlow ordered as she approached with two other officers.

I had reason to swallow the lump in my throat now. Whatever was about to happen wouldn't be good.

We didn't get the chance to say goodbye to Velma or Yolanda as we were cuffed, heavy hands on our arms as we were escorted back inside.

"What is this about?" I demanded.

"Tell it to the warden," Barlow said.

I glimpsed Eleanor's sad eyes as she teared up. "What does the warden want with us?" I asked.

"We cleaned her office the best we could," Eleanor pleaded.

"Silence," an officer said.

They led us into the warden's office and stopped us before her desk.

Warden Geyer put down her pen and stared up at us. "What do you have to say for yourselves?"

"I thought we did a good job cleaning your

office," I said.

"I think you forgot to wipe her desk clean, Agnes," Eleanor said.

"Thanks, Eleanor, but it was our first day cleaning."

Warden Geyer pushed herself up from her desk as the intercom came on announcing that all inmates were to return to their cells for lockdown.

"This isn't about how you cleaned my office. It's about the murder of trustee Maria Lopez."

If a chair had been available, I would have collapsed into it. "I don't understand. We only spoke to Lopez when she replaced Officer Barlow."

"And only for a moment," Eleanor added. "She told us she was going to the warden's lounge."

I glared at Eleanor for revealing anything a fellow inmate had told us. "But when we knocked on the door later she didn't answer, and the door was locked. I wasn't even sure that was the right door."

"Perhaps you can show us, then," Warden Geyer said.

I shrugged and led the way from the warden's office to the door we thought was the lounge. The door was now wide open and the room crowded with deputies. "What's going on in there?" I asked.

"Why don't you take a closer look," Geyer said.

Eleanor and I walked into the room, which contained leather furniture, a television and a table near a window with a microwave on it. When we finally were able to move past the line of officers, we saw Maria Lopez's body sprawled on the floor.

"Oh no! Who would do this to Lopez?" I asked.

"That's what I thought you could tell us," Geyer said. "I can't imagine what you were trying to hide here that was worth murdering Lopez."

"We didn't kill her," I protested. "And how sure can you be that Lopez was murdered? That would require an autopsy."

"You can plainly see the bruises on Lopez's neck," Geyer pointed out.

"I'm sure you know that neither of us has the strength to strangle anyone. I have arthritis in my hands."

"Me, too," Eleanor proclaimed.

"How convenient," Geyer said, never breaking her composure.

"We'd be the least likely of suspects. Officer Barlow was supposed to be watching us while we cleaned."

"But she suddenly disappeared," Eleanor added. "Lopez told us that Barlow went to a meeting."

"And Doctor Franks disappeared, too," I said. "Wherever Barlow and Franks were, they came back together."

"So they weren't here when you killed Lopez?"

"We didn't kill Lopez! Why don't you check your camera," I said. "We've never been in this room before now."

"I don't have to review the tapes because I know who the guilty party is."

"Good, because it's not us," I insisted. "It's nice that you can't review the tapes for our benefit, only for your own."

"That's messed up!" Eleanor exclaimed.

"I want them both searched and taken to solitary," Geyer ordered the officers.

"So was there really a meeting today?" I shouted over my shoulder as the officers pulled us from the room. "And why wasn't anyone else up here today!"

Chapter Five

If I thought the mattress and accommodations in our cell were bad, they were four-star compared with the thin pads in solitary. I didn't mind the search, but I was glad I had ditched whatever was in that baggy I found buried in my cornbread.

Why did Jana give me the drugs? Did she think I was up for something like that? Was she trying to set me up? Was she hoping I'd get into an altercation with Crusher? I'm too old for fighting, and I've never struck anyone, including my children.

A small mesh window, currently closed, was set in the door. I presumed that allowed officers to check on me and speak to me. A thin slot at the bottom of the door was presumably how food trays would be given to me. This was beyond miserable.

I wanted to scream Eleanor's name to see if she was celled nearby, but we were now suspects in the murder of a trustee. It wasn't time to act out of line. I hoped that the security cameras would be checked, but I had my doubts that the warden had listened to anything we'd said.

In a mad panic I wondered whether Eleanor and I would be stuck here forever. I wished I had told Andrew where we were going. In fact, nobody other than Sheriff Peterson knew where we were or what we'd be doing. At what point would he contact our families? He had given us a month to investigate this case

I eased down on what served as my bunk, thumping my head on the wall. As I rubbed the back of my head, I heard a thump in return.

"Eleanor, is that you?" I called out finally. To hell with the guards. I couldn't imagine how frightened Eleanor would be about now.

I didn't get the response I wanted. Perhaps it would be better to call through the window. Surely there had to be some cracks that would allow sound to carry.

I stood up and stretched with a crack in my back. It sounded louder than usual, but in this place the echo was massive.

"Eleanor," I called out again.

"Agnes?" came Eleanor's voice faintly.

"I'm happy you can hear me. I hope you're okay."

"Good enough, I suppose, but I hate the accommodations."

She laughed loud enough for me to hear, which brought me some relief. At least her spirits were up. I had imagined Eleanor near tears, which I must admit was my first inclination when they put me in here.

"Settle down, you two," a woman's voice ordered. "The guards will be making a pass soon."

I heard footsteps approaching. I stumbled back at the sound of metal doors opening and slamming. When my window opened, Officer Schulze looked in on me.

"How you faring, Barton?"

"Well as expected, I suppose. I didn't kill .... ."

"We'll talk later. With any luck you'll be out of here soon. Lucky for you, the deputy director is still in town."

She had given me something to hope for. Would the presence of the deputy director pressure the warden to review the camera recordings?

I reclined on my bunk. In the corner, a fly continually bounced into the wall, lulling me into a light slumber.

I woke with a start at the clanging of metal. I couldn't tell how close it was, and the only voices were muffled.

I was blinded by light as my door opened and the frame of a man filled the opening. "Barton, it's time to go."

Eleanor was in the hallway behind the man. "I'm not sure if you remember me. I'm Deputy Director Smith. I saw you the first day in the chow hall. I hope you're getting along better with Officer Schulze. She's one of a kind."

"I know. I think that's why we butted heads, but it's hard enough in here without breaking the rules."

"Come along, then. The warden is expecting us."

We walked with Smith and I smiled at Eleanor. I was so happy to be released from solitary that I could kiss my friend. Eleanor and I are the closest of friends. I know as long as we're together we can get through anything, including incarceration, even if our stay is temporary.

Warden Geyer didn't look happy to see us when we walked into her office.

"It appears I've made a rush to judgment. The camera recordings show you both working diligently. But as you can imagine, it did look bad that you were the last ones here."

"Where was everyone earlier today?" I asked. "Was there really a meeting?"

"Potluck in the officer's lounge."

"Which is a violation of prison rules," Smith interjected. "You'll do well to remember to review cameras before you throw inmates in solitary. I'll assume you've already lifted lockdown. I'm sure you know how bad that is on the inmates. It stirs them up, and we can't afford that. It's bad enough that beautician was found dead. What have you found on that front? Any suspects?"

"I-I hardly think this is the time to talk … ."

"Come now, Felicia. Certainly you can't be worried about what a couple of inmates might think of you. Especially after the camera fiasco."

"No, no suspects, but plenty of persons of interest … like the entire F Pod population."

"I hope you're also considering officers since Trudy was found during a lockdown," I pointed out.

"Do I really have to listen to inmates tell me how to conduct an investigation into something that happened before either of them arrived?"

"Of course not," Smith said, "but I wanted to point out what the inmates really think. They believe an officer is involved in Trudy's murder. The longer this case goes unsolved, the worse it will go for you."

"I understand that, but right now I have another investigation to conduct. I have no idea who would murder Lopez. She was well liked by inmates and staff."

* * *

The silence was thick when Eleanor and I returned to the pod. All eyes were on us. Eleanor waved and did a little jig. "I knew they wouldn't keep us long," she exclaimed.

I smiled as Char approached. "They wouldn't tell us what was going on. Let's meet in the shower room. They don't have cameras in there."

Eleanor and I gathered our toiletries and towels and headed for the showers. Crusher was standing by the sinks. She turned her head and glared at me. "Don't think I've forgotten what you did to me," she said with a clenched fist.

"I'm not looking for trouble. Next time I'll give you the cornbread, I promise. I wasn't aware why you really wanted it."

My heart pounded as Crusher rose to her full

height of nearly six feet. I feared I was about to die, but more inmates piled into the room, eager to hear our story. Char and Jessy led the pack, and all of them carried shower supplies. I knew I didn't have much time before a guard showed up.

I took a breath and dove in, "Maria Lopez is dead."

Gasps echoed off the tiled walls. "How?" Char asked.

"She was found dead in the warden's lounge."

"And the warden tried to put the blame on us because we were cleaning the offices today," Eleanor added.

"Lopez took over for Barlow, who was supervising us. She told us she was headed to the lounge, and that's the last time we saw her," I said.

"Why did you kill, Lopez?" Crusher asked with a sneer. "Kinda strange you two showing up in the pod and suddenly Lopez is murdered, just like Trudy."

The women murmured among themselves.

"I assure you we have no reason to kill anyone.

We liked Lopez. She told us about Trudy's death." I sighed. "And when the warden checked the cameras, they proved that we were only cleaning. The recordings must have shown that we never entered the lounge when we were searching for Lopez. We knocked on the door, but it was locked."

"How did you get the warden to check the cameras?" Velma asked.

"She wouldn't. Instead she put us in solitary."

"Lucky for us, the deputy director was still in town," Eleanor said. "He made the warden check the cameras."

"This entire thing doesn't add up," I said. "First, Barlow insisted she had to stay with us the entire time we were cleaning."

"And then she disappeared, supposedly to a meeting," Eleanor added. "That's what Lopez told us, anyway."

"Then Dr. Franks must have joined Barlow, because later they returned together."

Yolanda's nostrils flared slightly. "So they couldn't have murdered Lopez."

"I'm not sure. They could have murdered Lopez after we came back to the pod," Eleanor said.

"Or Barlow," I pointed out. "Dr. Franks brought us back to the pod, remember?"

"You're right. Barlow also told us the warden was off today, but she returned."

"She would have to with the discovery of a body," Velma said.

"Does anyone know how Trudy died?"

"Why does that matter?" Char asked.

"I was wondering whether it was the same way Lopez was murdered. She was strangled. She had bruises on her neck."

"I don't know how Trudy's died," Yolanda said.

"She didn't have any bruises on her neck that you could see?"

"Not that I noticed, but we were all pretty upset at the time."

"I can imagine. There's no way the warden would share the findings of the autopsy with us."

"You certainly know a lot about how things work," Jessy said. "Are you a cop?"

"Not hardly, but Lopez told me about how upset the inmates were about losing the beautician. Were you really planning to riot over it?"

"Some good that threat did," Yolanda said.

"So you never planned to go through with it?" I asked.

"No."

"Of course we could stage a little sit down over Lopez's murder," I suggested.

"What's going on in here?" an African-American inmate asked as she pushed her way into the shower room. "I didn't call a meeting today."

"Mary, Lopez was murdered in the warden's lounge," Yolanda said. She then brought Mary up to speed.

"Lopez too? It seems we might all need to watch our backs."

I stared at Mary who wasn't necessarily an imposing person. But from the way she pursed her lips and folded her arms across her chest, I just knew she was someone of great importance in the pod. She also had two other inmates with her who might just be the muscles of her operation.

I introduced myself to Mary, "I'm Agnes, and this is Eleanor."

Mary rolled her eyes. "You don't have to introduce yourself to me, honey. I know everything that goes on in this pod. Whatever you girls plan to do, keep me out of it. Just don't get us locked down. I can't do business that way."

I was relieved when Mary left, until Yolanda said, "You really need to be careful. Mary Phelps is the pod's dealer."

"Agnes doesn't care about that," Crusher laughed. "I just hope you ladies know that Agnes and Eleanor here won't be able to do anything in the way of finding out who murdered Trudy and Lopez. You're all fools if you believe otherwise."

I waited until Crusher left the room. "We do need to do something like a sit down or hunger strike."

"Hunger strike?" Eleanor said. "I've been hungry since I've been here. Doesn't this prison ever serve anything edible?"

"No, that's what commissary is for," Yolanda said. "You'd be surprised what we can whip up. We should get our chance to go later."

"The only problem with staging a protest," Velma said, "is that we could be put on punishment and lose privileges. A loss of commissary wouldn't go over well with anyone."

"What suggestions do any of you have then about forcing the warden to allow me and Eleanor to investigate the deaths of Trudy and Lopez?"

"You can't force that dragon lady to do anything," Char said.

"I can see that, but do we have your support to speak on your behalf. The warden is worried you might riot over the death of Trudy. And I believe she might give Eleanor and me the permission to investigate the deaths if it's spun the right way."

"Can't you do that without the warden?" Yolanda asked.

"We could if it was only us inmates we're talking about. But we need the freedom to question the guards, too."

"She'll never give you the permission to do that. Everyone knows how close-lipped the officers can be."

"Not to worry. We have experience about how to extract information from people who refuse to cooperate," Eleanor said with a wink.

"I think you're both crazy, but what do we have to lose," Char said. "When will you put your plan into motion?"

"After commissary would be good because we don't know whether the warden will yank our privileges."

Chapter Six

Eleanor and I, along with Char, Yolanda, Jessy and Velma, walked to the commissary. I chose Snickers candy bars because sweets made me happy —most of the time.

"How much can we spend?" Eleanor asked.

"Thirty-seven dollars a week," Yolanda said.

"I'm not sure how much of that I want to spend on pop."

"You can buy a pop card. That will cost you two dollars and fifty cents."

Eleanor's face came alive. "You mean I can get as much pop as I want for that?"

Yolanda laughed. "No, that would be per pop."

"That's a total rip off," Eleanor complained, "but I do love my Diet Coke." Eleanor grabbed a fistful of pop cards.

"So that's all you plan to buy?" Char asked. "You won't have any money left to buy anything else."

I helped Eleanor put most of the pop cards back and picked up a candy bar, waving it in her face. "Yes, like a candy bar. I know how much you love them." I picked up apple cinnamon oatmeal. "I'm getting Hawaiian Punch; it's cheaper."

Eleanor wandered along another snack aisle. "This is actually fun."

"Prison isn't all doom and gloom," Velma said. "Commissary keeps us sane."

I stared at Eleanor's hand basket, which she was filling with banana Moon Pies. Before I had the chance to say anything, she asked, "What? I hope you don't plan to deprive me of these Moon Pies."

"No, I just thought you might want something more sensible, like granola bars."

Eleanor eyeballed my basket. "I can't help but notice you don't have any granola bars in you basket, Agnes."

I chuckled to myself. "I hope I have enough

money in my account for all of this."

"I hope so, too," Jessy said. "It would be embarrassing if you don't."

I glared at Jessy as she passed in front of us. She then stumbled and crashed to the floor, several cans of ravioli thumping her on the head. She jumped up instantly. "Which one of you old bats tripped me?"

I backed up. "Don't look at me."

"She means don't look at us," Eleanor quickly added. "You should watch where you're walking."

"Or who you're antagonizing," Char said with a wink. "I have a feeling Agnes will be running our pod soon."

I shook my head and piled my items on the counter. I gave the man behind the counter my pin number and he checked the computer, supposedly to make sure I had funds for my purchase. He then rang up my items and put them into a paper bag. "Luckily someone deposited money into your account today," he said.

I lingered close to the counter as the man rang

up Eleanor's purchases. He told her the same thing.

"Who could have deposited money into our accounts?" I asked Eleanor. "Nobody knows we're here."

"Beats me, but I'm glad they did, whoever it was."

"Huh!" Jessy said, moving past us.

"What's wrong with her?" I said.

"I think she's still miffed about her little fall," Char said.

"I can't believe you ladies actually tripped her up," Yolanda said with a grin. "I've wanted to do that for a long time."

"Jessy told us she's been in here before," I said.

"Yes, and she was miserable that time, too. That one is a trouble maker," Velma said. "I'm sure by the time we get back to the pod she'll have some conspiracy worked up in her head."

"We didn't do anything to her. She's the one who chooses to be a shrew to us."

"Prison isn't much different than high school at times," Yolanda admitted. "Or a college dorm."

"So how did you wind up here?" I asked Yolanda.

"My boyfriend asked me to deliver drugs to this guy a couple of times. I don't know why I did it, but the cops caught up to me and I was arrested. The thing was, I had gotten away from that loser and had just enrolled in college classes. I wanted to be a nurse, but now that's all gone. I'm serving a thirty-year sentence."

I shook my head. "That seems a long time for delivering drugs a few times."

"That's what my mother says, but I should have taken the plea or waited for a better one."

"You never take the first one they offer," Char said. "It's hard to know what to do when you're young. Ninety percent of the people here deserve to be here, the other ten percent just made a mistake."

Yolanda wiped away the tears that rolled down her cheeks. "I'm taking classes here," she said. "I can earn a nursing degree and work in the sick room here, Dr. Franks said."

"I only met him briefly. Does he follow through with what he says?" I asked.

"He might be only the psychiatrist, but he did help me fill out the forms for the classes."

I nodded, although I had Dr. Franks on my suspect list along with Officer Barlow.

We were shocked to discover a television had been delivered to our cell. I hoped we weren't shown any special privileges. I was already nervous about the money deposited into our accounts. Was someone setting us up?

"Nice television," Char said from the door. "I was wondering when they'd bring that to you. All of the cells have them, although the television is cut off at midnight. It helps you keep sane."

"Next time I'll make better choices with my commissary purchases."

"I could share a few with you, maybe later. I hope you put your plans into motion. The entire pod is counting on you girls."

Eleanor waited until Char left before asking, "Just how are we going to do that?"

"We'll have to ask to see the warden," I said.

"I hardly think we'll be allowed to see her again today. She has a case to solve now."

"Yes, but I imagine she'll be happy to learn how we can help her."

"If she allows us to. I'm not so certain about this plan of yours. I think we'll be wasting our time."

"That doesn't sound like the Eleanor I know. The one I know is keen on a plan that will put us one step closer to solving a case."

"Except that we're not on a case. We're locked in here as prisoners." Eleanor frowned. "You know I'll go along with anything you say."

"We work as a team, remember? I can't do this without you."

"I'm glad to hear you say that, Agnes. It never gets old."

I eased down on my bunk until I heard a door open and close, alerting me that an officer was entering for a check. I hurried outside the door, frowning at the sight of Officer Barlow.

I stepped toward her. "Can I help you, Barton?" she asked with a cocked brow.

"Yes. We'd like to see the warden."

She rolled her eyes. "Of course, but I'm not certain she's here still."

"With a recent murder, I'm counting on her still being here. I have information."

"You can tell me. I'd be happy to take your message to the warden."

"I'm certain you would, but perhaps we should speak to the deputy director instead. He told us to contact him if I had any information." I put a hand against my cheek. "You know about preventing a riot."

"Snitch," Jessy shouted. She was watching us from her cell.

I glared at her as Barlow ushered us through the door that would eventually lead us to the warden's office.

Warden Geyer was standing in the doorway of the lounge. She looked over at us and said, "I didn't call you."

"I know, but the deputy director told us to speak with you if we remembered anything about earlier today."

"Should I take them back to their pod?" Barlow asked.

"No, I'll see them in my office. I'm sure it won't take long."

We followed the warden into her office and stood while she wearily sat behind her desk. "What's so important that you had to rush back here? You had plenty of time earlier when you had the undivided attention of the deputy director."

"Actually I was hoping to make a deal of sorts with you. The inmates are very upset about Lopez's death."

"You told them?" she asked as she stood with a reddened face.

"I had no choice. They would have eventually noticed Lopez missing."

"They were already threatening a riot with the death of the beautician. I can't even imagine what they'll do with another inmate murdered," I suggested. "She was well respected from what I've heard. If Eleanor and I were allowed to investigate the murders, I believe we could convince them to remain calm."

Warden Geyer fell back in her chair, laughing. "You have to be kidding? What could you possibly find out that trained law enforcement members can't?"

"Well, for one, the inmates would talk to us, but we need more than that. We need to know how Trudy was murdered."

"We also need to be allowed to question the officers," Eleanor said.

"Is that all? Should we all be considered suspects?"

"At this point, everyone is a suspect until we can narrow the choices. But we can't do that unless you allow us to help with the investigations."

"This is unprecedented. You're in here for armed robbery. Why do you want to change the tables? I hope you know the inmates will think you no more than snitches if I allow you to do this."

"I really don't care at this point. We need to solve the murders before the killer strikes again. Perhaps next time it won't be an inmate. Do you want that on your shoulders?"

"I think this entire thing is ludicrous, but I'll run it past the deputy director. Now get back to your pod."

In the pod, I walked right up to Jessy, who was shouting and pointing.

"Would you calm yourself," I said. "I already told you I wanted to ask the warden for permission to investigate the murders. That's hardly snitching."

"I, for one, would like to hear what they have to say," Mary said from a nearby table. "So what did the warden say?"

"After she laughed uncontrollably?" Eleanor asked.

"She told us she'd have to run it past the deputy director."

"Why ask for the warden's permission?" Mary asked.

"We need to question the guards and find out if Trudy and Lopez were killed in the same manner."

"You already told us that," Jessy said.

"But I missed that part," Mary said. "Sit yourself down, Jessy, and quit causing problems."

"Why do we even care that Trudy and Lopez were murdered?" Jessy asked.

"So it doesn't bother you that a killer is murdering inmates?" Mary asked as she stood. "You have to sleep sometime you know."

Jessy shakily took her leave, and I smiled. "Thank you, Mary."

"And I'll thank you to stay out of my business. I had to deal with what happened at lunch. But if there's anything I'm good at, it's taking care of loose ends."

I wasn't sure what she meant, but I was sure I'd find out soon enough as inmates began milling near the entry to the chow hall.

"That woman scares me," Eleanor admitted.

"Me, too, but at least she called off Jessy for the moment. We won't be able to do anything with her in the way. I'd rather not be invited to a blanket party."

"Blanket party?"

"They throw a blanket over you from behind and beat the hell out of you," said an inmate who stood near. "I can't imagine anyone would do that to either of you. Not with Char and now Mary looking out for you. We all hope the warden accepts your offer."

"Thank you. I didn't catch your name."

"Just call me Darcy."

Darcy had raven hair and the bluest eyes. While she carried some weight, she had the cutest dimples.

The door opened and we followed the line into the chow hall. Teresa was serving at the steam table, but Jana, the woman who had given me the cornbread, was missing. I didn't comment on it, but I felt something wasn't right. Did Mary exact her revenge on Jana for giving me the cornbread instead of Crusher?

Eleanor and I sat with Char, Yolanda and

Velma.

Char looked down at her tray. “I should have known it would be chicken. That’s all they ever give us, fish or chicken.”

“At least the chicken doesn’t look like it’s going to crawl back off your tray,” I said. I took a bite and made a face. “They certainly could learn how to use spices. This is the blandest thing I’ve ever eaten.”

“At least you have a candy bar for dessert,” Yolanda said.

“I miss eating candy,” Velma complained. “This diabetic thing is for the birds.”

“How well is your sugar managed here?” I asked.

“It’s a pain because Barlow was trained to check my sugar and give me my insulin. She refuses to let me give myself my own injections. I’m hardly going to run off with the needle.”

I nodded in understanding. “What do they do if you get sick?”

“We might be sent to see the doctor if we’re

knocking on death's door," Velma said.

"Is anyone ever sent to the hospital?"

"Only in emergency situations. People on the outside think we're taken good care of medically, but they'd be shocked at just how hard it can be to get the proper care."

I thumped my fingers on the table. It certainly was eye opening to be on the inside. I was beginning to get close to some of the inmates, and it was hard to believe they all had been convicted of crimes. Of course, being nice was no real indication.

"Have you seen Laura Keelie recently?" I asked Char. "You know, the sweet young thing who was in quarantine with us."

"Oh, you mean the one who murdered her grandparents."

I about swallowed my uppers. "Are you serious?"

"Why would I lie about something like that?"

"I didn't mean it like that. I'm just shocked."

"It doesn't shock me," Eleanor said. "I could tell

all that sweetness was an act."

I shook my head. Leave it to Eleanor to say that. I suppose I wasn't the best judge of character. I'd rather cut everyone some slack unless they gave me reason to think otherwise.

Chapter Seven

I left the chow hall earlier than the other inmates and returned to our cell. Even Eleanor stayed behind, talking with Char. We both had grown to like her. She was a great source of information and helped us learn the ropes.

I gathered the supplies to take care of my dentures and headed into the shower room. I had set my bag down and readied my denture cup when I spotted Jana wiping her face in front of the far sink. I smiled and walked over to her.

"Hello. I missed you at dinner."

"I wasn't feeling well, so they let me skip tonight," she said without looking up.

"Are you sure you're okay? I can't help but wonder if you were given any problems for giving me that cornbread at lunch."

She looked over at me and I noticed the black eye. “I don’t know what made me do it, but I couldn’t resist. I can’t stand Crusher. But I see you handled it well.”

“I’m not sure I’d say that exactly, but at least she didn’t crush me — at least not yet.”

“I knew I wasn’t supposed to touch that cornbread, but it makes me so angry that Mary is able to intimidate the kitchen staff to do her bidding.”

I nodded. “I don’t think Mary is someone to mess with. She certainly sounds nice and agreeable when she wants to, but when she said that she’d take care of what happened at lunch I just knew it spelled trouble for you.”

“I can hold my own, so no worries. From what I hear, you’re moving up in this pod. You might want to be careful. There are inmates who don’t like to see newcomers moving up the ranks so quickly.”

“I don’t care for any rank. All I want to do is find out who killed Trudy and Lopez.”

"I heard all about that, too. My advice is not to trust anyone, including me. It can be a deadly mistake in this place."

"I don't suppose you've seen another new inmate, Laura Keelie, have you? She's blond and just an itty-bitty thing. She came in the same day I did."

"Why, do you know her or something?"

"Not really. I just haven't seen her since the day we came into the pod."

"I'm certain she's somewhere. They treat missing inmates seriously around here."

"Have a good night, Jana," I said, moving back to where I was cleaning my teeth. It bothered me to think the poor woman had been beaten for giving me that cornbread. After I finished our stint here, I'd find a way to end Mary's reign of terror.

I was asleep when Eleanor finally came into the cell at count time, making all kinds of racket.

"Do you mind," I said, covering my head with the blanket.

"Don't be such a fuddy-duddy. If you had stayed

longer you could have played cards with us."

"I was too busy talking with Jana. She's the one who gave me that cornbread. Anyway, she has a black eye, thanks to Mary."

"She should have known better. But you should be glad you ditched those pills before you were caught with them."

"That's no reason to want to see a woman harmed for a mistake," I said, sitting up.

"In case you haven't noticed, this place is full of people who have made mistakes."

"I know that, Eleanor. I just feel bad for Jana."

"We should be careful whom we befriend. We have to watch our step."

"I know that, but it's hard not to be friendly with some of the inmates. It will help us fit in. Besides, we're already becoming friends with Char, Yolanda and Velma. Jana told me not to trust anyone, including her, though. What do you think, Eleanor?"

"I think we should be careful. Anyone could have murdered Trudy or Lopez."

"The staff sure looks good for it."

"Yes, but you know how it can go. Just when we think we have it all figured out, along comes a twist we never expected."

"That's what I'm worried about. I'm still wondering where Laura went off to."

"You mean the woman who killed her grandparents? That's the last person we should worry about."

"I suppose, but where did she go?"

"Well, I'm too tired to care now," Eleanor said, climbing into her bunk. We can ask around in the morning."

"If we're not investigating the murders."

"You don't really think the warden will let us do that, do you?"

"I don't know, but I hope so. We have to question those guards, especially Barlow."

"You seem like you've already made up your mind."

"I wouldn't feel that way if Barlow hadn't disappeared like she had when we were cleaning the offices. She was supposedly in the lounge eating a potluck?"

"I recall smelling food now that I think about it," Eleanor said.

I flipped over onto my stomach and said, "See that's another thing. If Dr. Franks and Officer Barlow went to the lounge, who else was there?"

"I suppose we won't find out unless we're given the chance to investigate."

I yawned as lockup was announced and our cell door slammed shut. It sent a tremor up my back. That metal on metal sound was enough to unnerve anyone. As I lay in the darkness, I could hear the murmuring of the other inmates. There was a tiny window at the top of our cell that barely allowed for a trickle of light to come in during the day. But in the dark, I felt lonelier than I've felt in a long time. I missed my Andrew and dreaded what would happen when he did find out where we were. I only hoped that Eleanor and I would be able to solve the case, and soon so that we could go home.

* * *

I showered while Eleanor made the beds. I enjoyed the hot water for all it was worth, and reached for where I had put my towel, but it was gone!

"Do you mind?" I asked loudly. I heard only heaving breathing. I tried not to panic, but that near silence had me wishing I had some sort of weapon. Throwing a shampoo bottle or bar of soap at someone would hardly do much good.

Someone tossed my towel to the bottom of my stall. By the time I picked it up, it was quite wet, which made me angry. The sound of footsteps receded from the showers before I could see who it was.

I dressed in a hurry, not even bothering to brush my hair, and raced back to my cell.

I was breathing hard and trembling a bit by the time I sat on my bunk.

"What's the matter with you, Agnes?" Eleanor asked. "You look a fright."

"I just wanted to hurry is all," I said. I didn't want to frighten Eleanor. Could it be that I was the only one of us targeted? I wondered how far it could escalate.

* * *

I took my breakfast tray to table where Eleanor, Char and Velma sat, scurrying around the table where Crusher hulked over her breakfast.

"I hope you're not letting that Crusher intimidate you, Agnes," Eleanor said.

"Easy for you to say. She's not angry with you."

"This has to do with the cornbread incident yesterday," Eleanor explained to the other inmates.

"Don't remind me. I really wish Jana had given Crusher the cornbread instead of me," I said. "I saw her in the shower room last night with quite the black eye."

"So that's why she isn't working today," Char said. "I should have known something like this would happen. You don't interfere in Mary's business."

"You think she's responsible?"

"Keep it down! Mary will have her girls mess

you up if she hears you talking about her," Yolanda hissed.

"I wish I had sugar for this oatmeal."

Yolanda pulled a few packets from her cleavage and slid them across the table to me.

"Thank you. I'll be sure to get sugar at the commissary next time."

"I was shocked they didn't have any bread yesterday," Velma said. "Now I have peanut butter, but no bread."

I nodded to Mary as she passed our table.

"Why did you do that?" Eleanor asked.

"I don't want to be on her bad side. She's the last person I want gunning for me."

"You're catching on," Char said.

Eleanor and I filed into the hallway to receive our job assignments. Barlow announced, "Barton and Mason, you're assigned to gather the trash today. I'll show you where to get the cart."

I gave Eleanor a look, and she merely shrugged. I kept silent for the moment though, because Barlow wouldn't have appreciated any backtalk.

Barlow led us into a room that housed two large gray carts with huge buckets that would accommodate multiple bags of trash. I glanced over to the large door that allowed a sliver of light to shine beneath it. "What do we do with the trash once the cart is full?"

"You can press that button over there," Barlow explained. "And put the trash into the Dumpster. It's not brain surgery."

I didn't appreciate her sarcasm. "I know that, but where are we supposed to collect the trash?"

"You'll find full bags in the kitchen, bathroom, showers and from the cells in the pod."

"Where we should start?" I asked Eleanor.

"Beats me, but we had better get moving, Barlow looks upset with us."

"You might want to start in the kitchen," Barlow suggested with a sly smile.

I didn't trust her change of attitude.

Once she walked away I said, "I was hoping the warden would have taken us up on our offer."

"Maybe she's still considering it."

"I suppose. I think Barlow is against us for suggesting she might have something to do with Lopez's murder."

"I have a feeling the warden told her what you said," Eleanor pointed out. "The officers and warden most likely stick together."

"I guess we'll have to investigate without the warden's permission."

"We won't be able to do much of anything other than question the inmates then. If the inmates try to rise up in protest, the warden will never give us the chance."

I nodded and rang the bell outside the locked kitchen door. Teresa answered the door with a roll of her eyes. Since she hadn't made a rude comment to us at the steam table this morning, I had thought she would be civil. But what do I know.

"We're here to pick up the trash."

That brought a smile to her face. "It's about time. The bags are leaking on the floor."

I sighed. I knew this wouldn't be a cushy gig.

The bags piled on the kitchen floor not only

leaked, they reeked. I tried to hold my breath as we picked the bags up and tossed them into the bin.

"Yuck," Eleanor said as she wiped the front of her shirt. "My clothes are filthy now."

"Mine, too, but I imagine that's what Barlow wanted to happen. Probably why she suggested that we come into the kitchen first."

"Or it could be because we have to clean up the kitchen sometime before we have to make lunch," Teresa said. "That is if you old bags ever get your cabooses in gear."

The other inmates in the kitchen stared at the three of us. I quickly noted the butcher knives chained to the stainless steel counters. I noted the chains were not nearly long enough to allow Teresa to grab one and reach us.

Once we had all the kitchen trash collected, we hurried from the kitchen.

I pushed one bin and Eleanor the other until we reached the back room. I pushed the button and the door rattled as it rose along the tracks. The Dumpsters were huge. There was no way we'd be able to throw the bags inside – the covers were closed and too high for either of us to reach.

Eleanor found and slid open a side door and we proceeded to sling the bags into the Dumpster. The bags continued to leak and the pungent aroma almost caused me to lose my breakfast.

Both of our hands were nasty. Only when we moved the emptied carts back in did I spot the box of gloves! "How nice that Barlow didn't tell us there were gloves," I said as I turned on the water at the sink.

"What do you expect? She's already proven to be an irritating officer. I wonder when Schulze will be back. I haven't seen her today," Eleanor mentioned.

"And here we thought Schulze was bad. I wonder if we should make nice with her. We need at least one guard that doesn't hate us."

"I'm not sure hate is the right word. Barlow has a job to do, but I can't imagine she thinks much of inmates. We're all guilty in her eyes," Eleanor said.

I sighed. "Except the only crime we've

committed is taking on this assignment."

Eleanor chuckled as she washed her hands after me. "Good! I thought I was the only one wishing we were back in Tawas."

We collected the many trash bags in the pod, some of which had been tossed from the second-floor cells. "At least these aren't leaking," I said.

"No, but some are certainly heavy," Eleanor replied.

When we went back to the Dumpster to toss this load, I heard voices on the other side a wooden fence. "I'm sorry, but I couldn't put a package in the dirty laundry this time," a man's voice said. "Someone else loaded the truck today."

"Well, you had better make darn sure you have something the next time. If the warden finds out what you've been doing, you'll have a cell all of your own to rot in the next thirty years," a woman threatened.

"That's Mary," I mouthed.

We slowly backed away. I was afraid to move until I no longer heard Mary's voice. The last thing

I wanted her to know was that we had overheard her conversation.

I led the way back inside and climbed the steps to the second level to make certain we hadn't missed any trash. I then met Eleanor at the bottom of the stairs. "There's nothing up there." I reported.

"Good, let's take a shower. You stink."

"I believe that aroma is both of us." I smiled.

Chapter Eight

I enjoyed standing under the hot water that surprisingly pounded my body with more pressure than I remembered. But that could be because I was the only one showering now, except for Eleanor, who was whistling in her stall.

I smiled as I lathered my hair until I heard a throat cleared. "Who gave you permission to take a shower now?" Barlow asked.

"I swear you told us after we were done picking up trash that we could shower. After all, you're aware how nasty those bags in the kitchen can be."

"Probably why you told us to go there first," Eleanor added.

"Hurry it up. The warden wants to speak with you."

Finally, I thought. We hurried and nearly

bumped heads when we flew out of our shower stalls. Eleanor and I dressed in a hurry and headed back to our cell, where we brushed our hair in a hurry before joining Barlow outside our cell.

She sighed and led us through the maze of corridors and locked barred doors until we came to the warden's office. Barlow escorted us inside, where Warden Geyer and Deputy Director Smith waited.

"You can leave, Barlow," Smith said. "I'll take them back after we're finished." Barlow reluctantly left, and Smith offered us chairs. "Please take a seat, ladies."

Geyer cleared her throat. "I should have called you earlier to my office, but Barlow informed me that you had already started your work assignment."

I tried my best not to double my fists. Barlow did that on purpose. "I see," I said, exchanging a look with Eleanor.

"Yes, the warden told me about your ... unorthodox ... proposal," Smith said. "I must tell you, that's just not done."

"That's what I told them," Geyer said.

"But under the circumstances, I don't think we have much of a choice."

"What?" Geyer exclaimed. "You could have filled me in before you told them that."

"I believe I had, in so many words. The truth is, we have a murderer loose in the prison."

"And it may not be an inmate since Lopez was murdered in the lounge," I added.

"Of course, we'll have to check that out to be certain," Eleanor said.

"The inmates seem to be comfortable about our investigation," I added, hoping to settle the warden down.

"I need to some assurances that you'll fairly investigate," Smith said. "While I'll allow you to interrogate the officers, I expect you to do the same with the inmates."

"I promise we'll do our best to find the murderer," I said. "We'll have to keep our conclusions to ourselves. To whom should we report?"

"You can tell me," Warden Geyer said.

"I'd rather they report to me, actually," Smith said. "After all, I'm the one who gave them permission to investigate."

"I still can't believe you're allowing this, but I'll go along with it. But I'm running this prison," Geyer said. "I'm certain you have more important things to attend to, deputy director."

"I've cleared my calendar. I want to be kept informed, and the only way that can happen is if I'm here. You'll have to tolerate my presence for a while longer, Felicia."

I noted the familiar way Smith referred to the warden, although I imagined that they had known each other for some time.

"We'd like to question the officers first," I said.

"Of course. Which ones?" Smith asked.

"Deputy Barlow and Dr. Franks. They were both here yesterday."

"Absolutely not!" the warden gasped.

"You promised me that you'd allow for an

impartial investigation, Felicia. And I'd appreciate it if you keep what's said in this office to yourself," Smith censured her.

"But what will I tell the officers?"

"That you have allowed for an independent investigation led by myself and Barton and Mason here. They have been selected by the inmates to look into the matter of the deaths of Trudy Taylor and Maria Lopez."

The warden sighed. "I'll need time to assemble the officers. They all have duties and as you know, we're understaffed."

"I'm sure Officers Schulze, Miller and Yates can look after the pod."

"Oh yes, we'd like to speak with Officer Yates, too," I said. "Sorry, I forgot until now."

"The warden will bring you to one of the offices after lunch. I'd also ask that neither of you tell the inmates what you find out in your investigation. If an inmate is the guilty party, it won't go well."

Barlow was waiting for us outside the door when we left the warden's office. I didn't smirk since it was enough that we'd be able to question her soon about the murder of Lopez.

* * *

We were the first ones to the steam table for lunch. Teresa wasn't there, but Jana's smiling face greeted us. I tried my best to not outright stare at her black eye, but the yellowing purple bruise was hard to avoid.

She scooped a creamy gravy filled with what I hoped was chicken over a biscuit. She also set a banana on our trays.

"This smells wonderful," I had to admit.

"Yes, we have a new chef. We're having vegetable lasagna for dinner."

"That sounds great — minus the vegetable part," Eleanor said.

We had our pick of the tables.

"How difficult do you think it will be to not tell the other inmates what we find out?" Eleanor asked.

"Very, although I think the less we say the better."

Char, Yolanda and Velma joined us as inmates filed into the chow hall. “I was wondering if we’d see you two,” Char said.

“Why wouldn’t you?”

“I just wondered what job you were given today.”

“We had to pick up all the trash,” I informed her.

“That’s a horrible job,” Yolanda declared with a shake of her head.

“I did that once and smelled like garbage for an entire week,” Velma insisted.

I smelled my arm just then and shrugged. “Barlow told us to empty the kitchen trash first.” I grimaced.

“It figures,” Yolanda said. “I think she gets her jollies out of giving us jobs like that.”

Velma took a sniff. “You must have gotten in a shower at least.”

“I’m not sure we were supposed to, but we took one anyway.”

“Barlow wasn’t around,” Eleanor added.

"So what did you do today, Char?" I asked.

"I always work in laundry because I'm the only one who seems to know how to use the sewing machine."

"I'm surprised they let you use one," I said.

"They post a guard in there, and believe me they count the needles."

"I believe someone ran the sewing machine while you were on the outside, Char," Velma said with a sly smile.

"Velma and me picked up trash in the yard. The warden might give us permission to plant flowers, but she hasn't given us the go ahead yet," Yolanda volunteered.

"That would certainly brighten up the place," I said.

After lunch the five of us walked outside for our yard time. I have a feeling there is safety in numbers. Still, it could have been anyone messing with my towel in the showers last night.

Mary was talking to a group of inmates who threw their arms skyward and stomped their feet.

"This is a bunch of bull," one of them shouted.

"It's out of my hands," Mary said, "and that's all I have to say about the matter. We'll all have to wait until next week."

I focused on the ground so as not to make eye contact with Mary. I picked up a few candy wrappers, depositing them into the trash can. I had thought that Yolanda and Velma cleaned the yard already. Perhaps they hadn't finished, or perhaps the inmates were slobs.

"Mary is getting flak now," Yolanda said. "I heard she didn't get her shipment."

"There are going to be a lot of pissed off inmates," Velma said.

"Serves them right," Char added. "If they get hooked on that garbage she peddles, that's what they get."

"We're talking drugs here, right?" I asked in a near whisper.

"Yeah, it's not hard to figure out."

I was shocked at Char's tone. "Don't you feel bad about inmates who are addicted to drugs?"

"Why should I?"

"Don't some of them rely on drugs to get by in here?"

"Drugs can be a physical addiction," Eleanor added.

"How do you two know so much about the subject?" Char shot back.

"You don't think we were straight when we decided to rob a bank and steal a car at our age do you?" I asked. "I'm ashamed to admit I became addicted to Oxycontin after a car accident," I lied. "It wasn't fun in jail trying to kick that stuff. I'm just glad that I did."

Char cocked a brow. "So you're saying what Mary does is fine in your book?"

"No, but I understand the dependency."

"What jail were you in anyway?"

Oh no, now I did it. "The Iosco County Jail."

Eleanor shot me a look, but I realized my mistake too late.

"Do you live in Iosco County?" Char asked suspiciously.

"No, we were just passing through."

"It seems like that would have been on the news. Two old ladies holding up a bank I mean."

"The sheriff there wanted to keep it quite because it's a tourist town," I insisted.

"So it happened in Tawas?" Yolanda asked. "My mother spends her summers in Tawas. It's no wonder the sheriff wanted to keep it quiet. My mother goes to Tawas to enjoy the crime-free atmosphere."

The loud tone signaling the end of yard time startled me. My heart was throbbing so hard that I thought they could all hear it. I might have made a blunder too big to recover from. If the inmates figured out who we really were, it might go bad for us. They'd find out we have helped put people behind bars!

Eleanor and I splashed water on our faces in the bathroom.

"Agnes .... ."

"I know."

We needed no other words. Eleanor was the

first person I made friends with when I moved to Iosco County. I only hoped we wouldn't meet our end in this prison.

We were reading in our cell when Schulze knocked on the open door and motioned for us to follow her. I was glad we had been summoned so soon after yard time. It would help if I could regroup.

Schulze led us into an office and then left with a stiff smile. We sat down and tried to relax, but I had an ache in my chest. Warden Geyer poked her head inside. "Officer Barlow will be right in."

"At least we don't have to wait long," I said.

"Who is leading the questioning?"

"I thought I could. You can jump in anytime you like."

"I like the sound of that."

The door opened and Officer Barlow dragged her feet all the way to the indicated chair. She interlaced her fingers until her knuckles loudly cracked while staring at me.

"Officer Barlow, thank you for coming," I

began.

"Like I had a choice."

"Very well, then. Tell us why Lopez took your place yesterday to watch over us?"

She leaned forward. "You made it clear that you didn't want me to supervise your work."

"Yes, but you also made it clear that's exactly what you planned to do."

"Why would you have an inmate oversee the work of another one?" Eleanor asked. "Do you have something to hide?"

"No," she growled. "Lopez is a trustee and has certain privileges. She often supervises other inmates."

"In the office area?" I asked.

Her eyebrows knitted. "I have no idea whether Lopez has supervised anyone in the office area before."

"Perhaps you should make a point of knowing," I suggested. "Isn't the warden's lounge kept locked?"

"Usually."

"Why wasn't it yesterday?" Eleanor demanded. "Who opened that door?"

My eyes widened at Eleanor's determined face without a hint of the familiar smile.

Barlow shook her head. "I knew this was a mistake."

Somehow I had to play good cop. "Just answer the question," I said kindly.

"Fine. So I might have unlocked the door for Lopez."

"Please be clear. You might have unlocked it or you did unlock it?" I asked.

"I can't remember."

"But that was only yesterday," Eleanor said. "How could you have forgotten a detail like that?"

Barlow folded her arms now. "I don't have to answer your questions. I'm over this," she said as she moved to stand.

"According to the deputy director you do. Of course, you're within your rights to speak with him about the matter. But I can't say it will go well for you. He gave us permission to question you," I said.

"I unlocked it for Lopez. Are you happy now?"

"No need to be hostile."

"I'd like to know why?" Eleanor asked, "if Lopez was supposed to supervise us in your stead."

"Because it's comfortable to sit in there. The warden always has doughnuts and coffee."

My eyes widened. "I was under the impression that the warden was out yesterday until Lopez's body was discovered."

"You'd have to ask her that. Good luck with that, by the way."

"Let's get back to you, Barlow. Where did you go when Lopez took over?"

"I went to the break room. We had a potluck yesterday."

"And did Dr. Franks go with you?"

"No."

"But you came back together," Eleanor pointed out.

"Yes, we walked up the hallway together. He always goes to his car for a cigarette break."

"I didn't think smoking was allowed on the

premises," I said.

"Rules like that aren't always followed," she admitted.

"Unless those rules apply to the inmates."

"Of course. You do know inmates are here for committing crimes, right?"

"I know that. I was only trying to establish what is allowed and what isn't."

"I'm not sure I'm buying your story," Eleanor said. "For all we know, you could have murdered Lopez when we were busy cleaning the offices. We never saw which way you went. You merely disappeared from our viewpoint."

"That doesn't make any sense. How wouldn't you have seen me sneak past you?" Barlow asked.

"Of course you could have murdered Lopez after we left for lunch when Dr. Franks took us back to the pod. Are you in this together?" I asked.

"No. What reason would I have to murder Lopez? She was handy to have around. There's never been a more trusted trustee. I counted on her."

"Yes, counted on her to not supervise two new inmates. I hope the warden allows me to take a look at your file."

Barlow's face reddened and her voice became louder. "My employee file is none of your business!"

"I don't understand why you're being so hostile."

"It might be because you're accusing me of killing Lopez, and I don't need inmates snooping in my file!"

Eleanor shook her head. "Do you have a record of aggression against inmates?"

"No!"

"I find that hard to believe."

"Believe what you'd like. In case you haven't noticed, I haven't jumped across the table at you yet!"

"Do you have a personal relationship with Dr. Franks?" I finally asked.

"So now we're in it together?"

"You might be. He takes us back and you move

in for the kill. Probably had plenty of time to off Lopez."

"I'm done with this for real this time. Tell the deputy director anything you like."

We watched as Officer Barlow stalked from the room and slammed the door.

Chapter Nine

Eleanor and I stood staring at the closed door, exchanging smiles.

"We certainly rattled her," I said.

"Yes, but I was thinking ... the lounge door was locked before Dr. Franks took us back to the pod."

"That's a valid point. And Barlow never mentioned anything about the door being relocked. Of course she still could have killed Lopez, I think. She could have hidden in the room or in another office."

Eleanor nodded. "So Officer Barlow isn't off our list yet?"

"No, but we need to speak with the warden about what the security camera by the lounge door captured."

Warden Geyer opened the door, frowning at us.

"You've certainly riled up Officer Barlow. She's asked to leave for the day."

"That's certainly suspect," I replied.

"No, I think it has something to do with what she might do to you if she saw you the rest of the day."

I laughed. "That's a little over-dramatic I think. Is that her M.O.?"

"Barlow is usually cool as iced tea. I've never known her to be rattled."

"Will we be able to speak with Dr. Franks and Officer Yates today?"

"Yes on Yates and no on Franks. He's out of the office until tomorrow," the warden said. "I'll send Yates right in. Fortunately she didn't witness Barlow's outburst."

The warden left, and Officer Yates walked in and sat down, placing her hands palms down on the desk. "The warden said you wanted to speak with me."

"Yes," I began, "we were wondering where you were yesterday after we checked out the cleaning supplies and cart?"

"Well, Barlow reminded me that there was a potluck and I thought I'd grab a plate and bring it back."

"You planned to eat in the storeroom?"

"Yes. I do it whenever there's an inmate cleaning the offices. I'm supposed to be here in case more supplies are needed."

"Why didn't you lock the storeroom?"

"I thought I had."

Eleanor shook her head. "That's a negative. The door was open when we put the cart away. We were wondering where you disappeared to."

"Oh? The lock must have jammed then. It happens sometimes. I told the warden about it, but it hasn't been fixed obviously."

"So you went to grab a plate," I commented. "Did anyone go with you?"

"Yes, I went with Officer Barlow."

"So you were together in the break room?"

"Yes, for part of the time anyway. She had to use the bathroom once."

"Is that in the break room or in the hallway?"

"In the hallway. We don't have a bathroom in the break room. The warden took that out and it's now a small locker room."

"I see. Since we didn't see you come back when we left, and Barlow and Dr. Franks returned before you, that creates a window of opportunity."

"Officer Barlow and Dr. Franks were talking in the hallway. I slipped back into the supply room before they came back. I wondered why the cleaning cart was in the supply room."

I glanced over to Eleanor and said, "Are you aware of Officer Barlow's rapport with the inmates?"

"I really can't say. The only time I've seen her interact with inmates is when she brings them to get the cleaning cart."

"I see. What do you know about the trustee Lopez?"

"I really haven't had much contact with her. Sorry."

"And how do you get along with Barlow?"

"I get along with all my co-workers."

"To the point where you'd lie for them?"

Yates pushed herself up. "No, that's not something I'd ever do. I don't care who murdered Lopez." She sighed. "What I mean is, I hope you find out who murdered her, but whether it's an inmate or one of the staff, they need to pay for what they did."

I eased back in my chair. "Thank you," I said. "We don't have any more questions."

Yates nodded and left.

"Yates must have come back to the supply room while we were looking for Lopez," Eleanor said. "That's probably why we didn't see her."

"That sounds plausible. Also, according to Yates, Franks and Barlow came back after her, so I'm not certain that Barlow had enough time to murder Lopez."

"Not if Barlow and Yates went to the break room together," Eleanor said.

We left the room and knocked on the warden's door. "Come in," she called out.

I followed Eleanor inside. "We appreciate all your help, Warden Geyer, but I have a few questions."

"Certainly, but I hope you're not planning to interrogate me."

That gave me pause, but I asked. "How good a view does the camera have of your lounge door?"

"I'm not certain. I'll have to get back to you on that."

"How did Barlow and Lopez get along?"

"Great. We all loved Lopez. I'm still shocked about her death."

Not too shocked that she'd shed a tear, though. "Are you positive that Lopez got along with all the staff?"

"I never heard Lopez complain about anything other than how we've been progressing on the investigation into Trudy's death. Solving that case was very important to her."

"And why was that?"

"Ah, of course you wouldn't know. Lopez and Trudy Taylor shared the same cell."

My eyes widened. Why hadn't someone mentioned that before? "That's certainly a detail we missed."

"Lopez told us about Trudy, but not that they shared a cell," Eleanor muttered.

The warden's brow shot up. "Oh, and what did Lopez tell you exactly?"

"Just that the beautician was found dead in the shower room," I said. I shot Eleanor a look to silence her before she added to what I said.

The warden glanced at her watch. "Is that all? I have an appointment."

"We have one last question for you. Are there any problems with the lock on the storeroom door?"

"Why are you asking me that?"

"It's just that the door wasn't locked when it should have been."

"I'll have to speak with maintenance about it."

"Are you saying you weren't aware of the lock not functioning or that you don't recall writing a work order to fix it?"

"I don't recall anyone tell me it wasn't working. I consider keeping a storeroom door unlocked a serious violation of the rules. I'll have to check on that before I leave."

"We'd like to question Officer Schulze and Dr. Franks tomorrow, perhaps after our work assignment."

"I'd appreciate that. It will look better to the inmates if you continue to work among them. If you ladies appear to stand out from the other inmates, it might spell trouble for you."

The warden grabbed her jacket and clear plastic bag. "I'll take you back. The deputy director had to leave unexpectedly."

Geyer walked us back to the pod.

We had taken no more than a few steps before inmates surrounded us.

"What happened?" Char asked.

"Why did the warden call you to her office?" Yolanda asked.

"If you remember, we made an offer the warden couldn't refuse yesterday."

Her eyes bulged. "Do you mean the warden actually gave you the permission to investigate Trudy's death?"

"Yes; I couldn't believe it myself."

"Let me guess," Mary began, "They want you to say an inmate killed her."

"She never said anything like that. Eleanor and I will be questioning staff and inmates alike."

"Are you saying the warden is actually going to allow you to question the officers?" Velma asked. "For real?"

"We already questioned a few, although we're not at liberty to tell you who. It's proven very interesting, to say the least. The warden doesn't want us to say too much on the matter, of course."

"I bet," Mary grumbled. "And what about Lopez?"

"My feeling is that the deaths are related," Eleanor said.

I sighed. I just knew this was going down the drain in record speed.

"All I can say is that two inmates have been

murdered and I think we all need to watch ourselves."

"I'd like to see them try to mess with me," Mary boasted.

"Of course, you have your girls with you all the time," Yolanda pointed out.

"You know it. Let's go Frankie and Midge. We have business to attend to."

"You don't plan on interfering with our investigation?" I had to ask.

"Nope, but don't think for a minute that I'll help either of you. I have more important things to do."

I was relieved when Mary left. I knew all about her important business, but I wasn't in the position to rat her out. Inmates don't tolerate snitches — but we won't always be in here.

Eleanor and I excused ourselves to relax in our cell before dinner.

"I think we told the other inmates too much," Eleanor said. "I hope the warden doesn't find out about it."

"It can't be helped now. She'll never hear it from us, and I can't imagine any of the inmates will tell her."

"We could have a snitch in our midst," Eleanor suggested.

"Let's hope not. Everything so far points to a member of the staff. There weren't any inmates in the offices when Lopez was murdered."

"True." Eleanor nodded in agreement.

"We'll have to check the door of the storeroom. I'm not sure I believe the warden had no knowledge that the lock is broken."

Crusher cruised slowly past our cell, rubbing her fist suggestively. I gulped hard and Eleanor asked, "What's the matter, Agnes?"

"My throat is getting sore is all."

"It looks like there's a line at the chow hall. We better get a move on before all the hot food is gone."

* * *

We sat down with our trays. Char sat at another table, but Yolanda and Velma joined us.

I glanced over at Char, who was speaking with Mary, and I couldn't help but wonder whether she was upset with us about our role as investigators.

"Don't worry about, Char," Yolanda said. "She's had a bug up her butt all day."

"About what?"

"Barlow cited her for insubordination. She has to talk to the warden about it tomorrow."

Velma laughed. "Yes, she told Barlow to go … ."

"No sense in finishing that sentence, Velma. We all would love to tell Barlow that," Yolanda commented.

"You could include me on that list," I said. "What did Barlow do?"

"Gave her extra duty for tonight. After lockup, if you can believe that."

"That doesn't sound safe. That should be against policy," I said. "Besides, I think Barlow left for the day after we questioned her." I grinned. "I don't think she much cares for inmates grilling her."

"That's what she deserves for giving us a crap

job today," Eleanor said. "I don't feel bad for Barlow."

"Let's not get too hasty. We didn't turn up anything on Barlow."

"Barlow used to be tolerable, at least until Felicia Geyer was appointed warden," Velma said.

"Was she promoted?" I asked.

"No. She's from the Ohio prison system. None of the officers took to her right away, but Barlow got along well with the last warden. Some say a little too well," Yolanda hinted.

"Did she have an affair with the last warden?" Eleanor asked with a grin.

"Allegedly," Velma put in. "Warden Jimmy Blair wasn't hard on the eyes." She winked.

Yolanda's eyes twinkled. "No, but he was married — with children,"

"I can see that Barlow might be upset about that revelation if she wasn't aware he was married. He might have given her privileges the sitting warden doesn't give her," Eleanor suggested.

"I love to gossip," I said. "But this doesn't have

anything to do with our investigation."

"The warden sticks up for her officers, from what we've seen," Eleanor added. "It's too bad we didn't get the chance to meet the nice Barlow."

"Or the tolerable one," I added. "But we'll just have to deal with her. Of course, she's not the only one we're considering."

We walked into the recreation room and Velma pulled out a board game. I sighed at the familiar Monopoly box.

"I'm not sure I'm up for Monopoly," I said.

Yolanda flashed a deck of cards and put them away. "We'll start the real game after Officer Miller does her check."

"I haven't seen her since we arrived."

"Probably not, but it's her shift tonight," Char said as she approached us.

"If you haven't spoken with Officer Miller yet, now is your chance." Yolanda said.

"I'm not sure the warden would approve of that. I have the feeling that she'd rather set up the interviews with the staff," I said.

Laura Keelie walked into the room accompanied by a few other inmates I'd seen around Mary.

"Laura seems to have broken out of her shell," I observed.

"Yes, a little to fast if you ask me," Char said.

"Meaning what?"

"She might be a plant."

"You always think that," Velma said. "Or you did the last time you were in here."

"A plant for what?" I asked.

"A cop for starters. She might be in here to bust up Mary's operation."

"Would that be a bad thing?" I asked.

"Of course it would be," Eleanor exclaimed. "Can you imagine how some inmates might react if they can't get their fix?"

"Eleanor is right. Bad enough some of them will have to wait it out until next week when the next shipment is due," Char said. "Unless they can get an officer to bring something in."

Chapter Ten

An officer would smuggle in drugs for the inmates? Why would any of them risk their freedom over that?

"Aren't they checked when they come into work?" I asked.

Eleanor gave me a kick under the table. "Has a cop ever been sent here undercover?" she asked.

"Actually, yes," Yolanda said.

"And she left in a body bag when the inmates found out about it," Velma said.

I willed myself to not swallow the lump that was forming.

I forced a smile. "It would be premature to assume Laura is anyone other than another inmate trying to fit in. She might even know one of the inmates. I saw her in the shower room our first night and she was sharing a cigarette with an inmate."

"Which one?" Char asked.

"I really couldn't say. I didn't look too closely and an officer was looking for me so I had to hightail it out of there."

"Good thinking on your part," Char said. "Enjoy your card game. I'm going to take it easy. I have late-night duty. I'm buffing the floors tonight."

"After lockup?" I asked.

"Yes, but don't worry about me. I'm tough as nails."

I sighed when Char left. "I wish I didn't have to worry about Char, but I have a sick feeling in my gut that won't quit," I acknowledged.

"I agree," Eleanor said. "Is that normal — to be given late-night duty?"

"They buff the floors once a month after lockup," Yolanda explained. "I don't think there's anything unusual with that."

"But since Trudy and Lopez's murder I'm just not sure of anything," Velma admitted.

Officer Miller nodded as she entered the room, looked around, and left. Yolanda then pulled out the cards and shuffled. "We're playing Texas Hold 'em."

"How do you play that?" I asked.

"You're dealt two cards and five are placed down face up on the table. You can use three of the cards on the table that go with the two cards you're dealt."

"I've played this online before," Eleanor said. "You know the basics of how to play poker, Agnes."

"What are we betting?"

Velma removed the paper money from the Monopoly game. "Each hand you win you'll be given a one dollar bill."

"Whoever accumulates five dollars first, the other three players owe them five dollars of purchases at our next commissary trip," Yolanda said.

"That works for me," Eleanor said.

I glanced one more time at Laura, who gave me a dirty look. I couldn't help but wonder if Char was right. Was Laura a cop planted to break up Mary's business? She certainly didn't look like an undercover cop, but neither did we.

I glanced at my cards. I had two aces, the makings of a good hand since an ace was also down on the table.

We each were given a turn and my three-of-a-kind aces high beat the three-of-kind twos that Yolanda had. I happily took my dollar winnings.

The next round Eleanor smiled as the cards were dealt and she claimed the next dollar when she set down two hearts that used the three hearts on the table. "I wish this was a real betting game," Eleanor exclaimed. "I have a feeling that I'm going to clean up."

Eleanor and I both frowned as we made way for our cell much later. "I think Yolanda is a card shark," I remarked.

"I think you're right."

I yawned. "I need to run to the bathroom before lockup," I said. "Are you coming, Eleanor?"

"I'll catch up. I need to look for my face lotion."

Because so many inmates were milling around I felt safe heading to the bathroom alone. The bathroom was empty, and I hurried into a stall.

I had no more sat down when someone knocked on my stall door. "This one is occupied," I said nervously. All I could think about was that I shouldn't have come to the bathroom alone.

The wall of the stall began to shake and I bit my fist. I yanked up my pants and pushed myself out.

My heart practically leapt out of my chest when the last stall door opened and Eleanor stepped out. "Why would you do something like that, Eleanor?"

"Do what?" she asked with a puzzled look.

I angrily washed my hands and marched back to my cell, where I readied my bed for lights out. I couldn't believe that Eleanor would scare me half out of my mind.

When Eleanor joined me in the cell, I turned my back to her.

"What's going on with you, Agnes?"

"You know what you did."

"If I knew I wouldn't have to ask you."

I sat up and glared at her. “And I suppose you’ll deny that you knocked on my stall door and rattled the walls while I was in there?”

Eleanor sighed. “Why would I do something like that? I know how much on edge you have been.”

“So you swear it wasn’t you?”

“Pinkie swear,” she said.

“Did you see anyone coming out of the bathroom when you were going in?”

“So someone scared you half to death in the bathroom?”

I simply nodded because I was overcome with emotion as tears burned the back of my eyes. “Neither of us are safe here, Eleanor.” I still didn’t want to tell her what had happened in the shower room. I now knew I was a target, but why? Would Crusher go to this extreme? I wasn’t certain, but I learned my lesson. I’ll never go anywhere without Eleanor at my side.

“I’m a little worried about Char,” I finally said. “What if she decides we might be cops, too?”

“I’ve thought about that, but so far she seems

to get along with us. We just need to keep her that way. We need to watch what we say, though, with her especially."

Officer Miller glanced into our cell and said, "Two minutes to lockup."

"I had no clue you worked nights in the pod," I said.

"What business is my schedule to you?"

"I didn't mean any offense."

Officer Miller didn't say a word as she walked away.

"It looks like I've overstepped my bounds once again. I just haven't a fix on her yet. She looked like a pushover in quarantine."

"That's our first mistake," Eleanor said. "At this point we don't know anything about the officers — or the inmates for that matter. Any of them might be the person responsible for the deaths."

"But how would an inmate have access to the shower area during lockup?"

"That's a question we'll have to ask tomorrow. If the warden tells us who was working the night

Trudy was murdered."

The cell doors closed with a resounding slam and the lights dimmed. It was the kind of sound that made my heart ache a little. I couldn't imagine how anyone could tolerate the atmosphere in the prison for long, especially lifers. Day in and day, out the same routine. The only thing that changes are the jobs you're given or the comings and goings of other inmates. The food is bland for the most part, fish and chicken the main staples.

I changed clothes in the near darkness and crawled into bed, drifting off to sleep not long after.

* * *

I woke to the glare of a flashlight and I glanced up as the officer moved past. In one of the cells directly across from me a woman waved a roll of toilet paper. I thought that odd, but I settled back in my bunk. Was it possible an inmate could be released during lockup?

"What's the matter?" Eleanor asked.

"There's someone waving a roll of toilet paper

in one of the cells across from us."

"Maybe she has to use the bathroom."

"Bathroom? I don't recall anyone telling us we could use the bathroom during the night."

"How could you? They told us so much that I couldn't even keep track of it all," Eleanor said.

I clambered out of my bunk and watched an officer open the woman's cell. The officer then escorted her to the bathroom.

I shook Eleanor all the way awake. "That's how it happened."

Eleanor wiped the sleep from her eyes. "How what happened?"

"How Trudy was let out of her cell during lockup."

"I thought we figured out a guard had to do it. That's how she was murdered ... by a guard."

"I don't think so. What if one officer let one inmate out to use the bathroom at the same time another inmate was let out by another guard? It sounds plausible doesn't it?"

"Yes, except that they must have been taken to

the bathroom by the guard. And watched, most likely."

I picked up a roll of toilet paper. "I'll find out," I said as I waved the roll between the bars.

"Thanks for ruining my sleep. I was dreaming about snuggling in bed with Mr. Wilson."

"Sorry, but we need to widen our scope. We can't be so one-sided that we miss the real killer."

"Then all you have to do is find out how an inmate killed Lopez when we were the only ones in the office area."

An officer approached. "I suppose you have to use the bathroom, too."

"Yes, is that a problem?"

She unlocked the cell and relocked it once I stood on the outside. I stared at her badge that read "Officer Greer."

She led me to the bathroom, where Officer Miller stood outside the door. "Make it snappy," Officer Greer said.

I hurried inside where another inmate stood at a sink.

"I can't believe they let us both use the bathroom," I said.

"Shhh," she responded. "They'll hear you."

I wanted to question the inmate, but I knew she was trying to hurry. I hurried myself since I did have to pee. When I came out of the stall the inmate was gone, but a white powder sparkled on the sink. I thought it might a drug, but I was too afraid to taste it.

"Are you finished yet?" Officer Greer asked as she walked into the bathroom.

I hurriedly washed my hands and flushed the white powder down the sink. That's all I'd need — to get a drug charge while I was in here.

Eleanor was snoring by the time I returned to the cell. I wanted to shake her awake, but I had already done that once tonight. It was hard for me to relax because I had something of interest to report. Ah heck, I'll just have to wait until morning.

Chapter Eleven

Eleanor and I headed to the shower in the morning without incident. “We need to send our clothes to laundry today,” Eleanor said.

We hurried back and bagged up our labeled clothing and put it in the laundry bin. By the time we were in chow hall, the line had all but diminished, and all that was left was thick, pasty oatmeal. None of the inmates we had come to know were at the tables.

“We should have gotten up earlier,” I said.

“If we had gotten up any earlier our cell door still wouldn’t have been open,” she reminded me.

“Yes, and there was a crowd ahead of us.”

“So what did you find out last night?” Eleanor asked.

“Apparently two officers do take separate

inmates to use the bathroom at the same time. While I was escorted there last night, the guards stayed outside. I wanted to ask the inmate I saw last night a few questions, but she told me to keep quiet."

"That makes sense. I'm sure you're not supposed to be conversing with another inmate on a bathroom run."

"You're not supposed to be doing drugs in there either," I pointed out.

Eleanor's mouth fell open. "What?"

"I need to find that inmate and ask her a few questions even if she doesn't want to. I know how to make her talk."

We walked to the hallway for our work assignments. "It's about time," Officer Schulze said. "I was worried that you two decided to fly the coop."

"Who, us?" I laughed. "It's not like that sort of thing happens."

"Let me just say that it's been attempted."

"How long have you worked here?" I asked.

"Too long, if you ask my mother, but seriously, ten years."

"Can I ask you a question?"

"Go ahead. The warden warned the officers that you would be asking us all a few questions."

"Did you work the day Trudy Taylor was found dead?"

"Yes, but I didn't get in until eight o'clock. But by that time the prison was on lockdown. I'm shocked they let me in, actually."

"I'm certain extra guards were needed."

"You might say that."

"Do you ever work nights?" Eleanor asked.

"Only if necessary, like if an officer doesn't show up. It hasn't happened in more than six months though. I have higher seniority than most of the other guards."

"Even Officer Barlow?" I asked.

"She's been here a year less than me."

"So did you work here when Warden Blair was in charge?"

"I imagine the other inmates told you wild

stories about Warden Blair and Officer Barlow." She laughed. "I think Barlow spread them, actually."

"So there's no truth to them?"

"No. Blair was a straight shooter. He was promoted to deputy director in Kent County. His family lives there."

"So it's not true Office Barlow used to be kind to the inmates?"

"Sure she was, until she found out how manipulative they can be. She was suspended when an inmate supposedly escaped on her watch."

"What do you mean, 'supposedly?'" I asked.

"Dora Roade was a prankster. She thought it would be funny to disappear for a few hours at lockup. And somehow Barlow didn't realize it until later. She's lucky she wasn't canned because it happened shortly after Warden Geyer's appointment."

"That sure would change an officer's attitude."

"I know she can come off as harsh sometimes,

but she's a good officer."

"So what were you told about the death of the beautician?"

"To not discuss it," Schulze said. "You'll have your hands full if you think you can sort out that mess."

"Mess?"

"The inmates all think one of the staff members are responsible and the officers think the same of the inmates."

"That much I figured out. What's the policy if an inmate needs to use the bathroom after lockup?"

"Agnes means besides waving the toilet paper."

"The inmate is escorted there and back," Schulze said.

"Do the officers wait in the bathroom?"

"We're supposed to."

"So if an officer doesn't, that could provide a window of opportunity that might have cost Trudy her life."

Schulze's brow rose sharply. "You say that like

you're not an inmate yourself."

I sighed. "You know, you're right."

"We're getting into this investigating thing," Eleanor admitted.

"It's too bad you didn't decide to work law enforcement instead of committing a crime."

"We've dabbled in crime solving, but more along the lines of finding a lost dog." I laughed.

"So what are our work assignments today?" I asked.

"You're off the hook for today. Your lawyers are here to speak with the both of you about your appeal."

"Lawyers?"

"Yes, don't you remember, dear, we arranged for them to meet with us once we settled in," Eleanor said.

"I'd hate to make them wait much longer then," I said, although my heart sank. If our lawyers are here, it means only one thing: that our husbands are here, which spells trouble for both of us.

We walked with Officer Schulze and stopped at a door labeled "Soundproof room." I took a breath as we entered, and Eleanor wiped at the tears that fell down her cheeks at seeing her frail husband, Mr. Wilson, who was seated at a table with my hubby Andrew.

"Have a seat," Andrew said.

We sat and it took a moment before I could look Andrew in the eye. "I know you must be worr … ."

"Save your breath. Sheriff Peterson gave us the scoop. Even Peterson was shocked that you two would want to be sent here in an undercover capacity," Andrew said.

"Shame on you, Eleanor, for going along with Agnes' scheme," Mr. Wilson chastised.

"You can't blame Agnes for that. We're partners and decided it was something we wanted to do. We just didn't know what we were getting into."

"Until we got here," I volunteered.

Andrew frowned. "How is the case going?"

"The warden gave us permission to question

the officers yesterday," I said. "But we've only had a chance to question a few."

"Hopefully today we'll get through a few more," Eleanor added.

"Then we'll be questioning a few inmates who knew the victim."

I moved my hand across the table and Andrew backed up. "You can't touch me. I have a reputation to uphold and a wife back home who thinks she's Superwoman."

"I hope that doesn't make me the sidekick," Eleanor said.

Andrew frowned. "So what is you backstory about how you two wound up here?"

"I robbed a bank." I winked.

"I stole a car and was the getaway driver," Eleanor added.

Andrew tried not to laugh, but he was doing a miserable job of it. "It's no wonder the bank in Tawas beefed up security." He frowned. "But seriously, you had better hope the other inmates don't find out who you really are."

"So far they don't. We're doing them all a service by trying to find out who killed the inmates."

"Inmates?"

Uh-oh.

"Oh, did we forget to tell you that another inmate was murdered, too?" Eleanor asked.

"I want you both out of here and soon," Andrew said.

"Yes, what he says," Wilson added.

"We can't until we've solved this case."

"How goes it with the other inmates?" Wilson asked. "Has someone made you their wife yet, Eleanor?"

"No, my heart and body belongs to Agnes."

I rolled my eyes. "That's the least of our worries. I'm glad you know now, Andrew. Once this case is solved we want out."

"I should teach you both a lesson and leave you here."

"I know you too well, dear. You'd never do that."

"No, but I wish you had spoken to me about what you planned to do."

"So you had a chance to talk me out of it?"

"No, so I could handcuff you to the bed." He winked.

"Oh, my," Eleanor exclaimed. "It's getting kinky in here."

"Seriously though, you're both in more danger than you know."

I thought about my shower and bathroom incidents. "I think we're aware of that."

"Now that we're allowed to question the officers, I'm certain we'll be able to solve this mystery," Eleanor declared.

"Is there anyone on the inside helping you out?" Andrew asked. "Like another law enforcement officer?"

"Not that I'm aware of, but we're trying to get chummy with one of the guards."

"I'm not sure that's wise; the killer could be one of the guards."

"I know, dear, but we need someone on our

side. The thing I worry about the most is one of the inmates who thinks everyone is a cop."

"You two should be ruled out," Mr. Wilson said. "You're both old enough to be grandmothers to most of the inmates."

"I'd rather not have you remind me of that," Eleanor said to Wilson.

He smiled instead of replying, and we stood when there was a knock at the door before Warden Geyer entered. "I wasn't aware it was visiting hours," she said.

"I'm her lawyer Andrew Hart and this is my partner Mr. Wilson."

The warden tried to hide her smile. "Okay then. I wanted to make sure this wasn't a social call."

"Our lawyers are working on our appeal," Eleanor said with a straight face.

"Don't you all. You can have more time if you need it."

"We're done now," I said as Eleanor and I left the room and closed the door behind us.

Chapter Twelve

"I hope you have Dr. Franks available for us to question," I said to Warden Geyer.

"Only one?"

"No, but Deputy Miller worked last night and I'm certain she went home to get some sleep."

"She's working overtime. Officer Barlow called in sick today."

"I'm sorry to hear that. Is it possible to see the guards' schedule the days Trudy and Lopez were murdered?"

"You should know who was working when Lopez was found dead."

"Officer Barlow and Yates?"

"Yes, that's right."

The warden led us into the room where Eleanor and I questioned Barlow and Yates the day before.

The aroma of coffee had my mouth watering. From the smell of it, I was certain that it would taste much better than what we get in the chow hall.

"Can we have a cup of coffee?"

"Help yourself."

The warden left and Eleanor poured the coffee.

"I wonder why she's being so nice," I said.

"I believe the warden is just as eager to have these cases solved as everyone else."

"Probably more since it happened on her watch."

We were stirring creamer into our coffees when Dr. Franks walked in the room, carrying a box of doughnuts.

My eyebrows shot up as he said, "I thought if I had to be in here being raked over the coals that I might as well brings some doughnuts." He smiled.

"Is that some kind of psycho babble?" Eleanor asked. "Trying to butter us up so we'll go easy on you?"

Dr. Franks sat down with the box still in his

hands. "Of course not, but I must admit I'm surprised that the warden is allowing you to interview the staff. I hope you also plan to speak with the inmates."

"I don't think I care for your tone," I said. "How about we ask the questions and you just answer them."

His face darkened. "No wonder Barlow called in sick today."

"I assure you it had nothing to do with us. Not unless it bothers her to be asked about the death of Lopez."

"There seems to be a lot of that going on," Eleanor said. "I know how people in your position might not understand inmates looking into the death of another inmate. As you might guess, inmates don't really trust officers and people in administration."

"I've been a psychiatrist for twenty years now and I'm not in the business of judging anyone, including inmates. I know the popular belief among the inmates is that the person who murdered Trudy Taylor is an officer."

"Is there something going on between you and Officer Barlow?" Eleanor asked.

Dr. Franks cleared his throat. "What does that have to do with the murders of Trudy Taylor and Lopez?"

"It might explain why you two left the office area when Eleanor and I were cleaning here. Barlow was quite insistent that we needed supervision."

"There was a potluck in the lounge room and I told Barlow to ask Lopez to look after you ladies."

"So it was your idea for Lopez to come up to the offices that day?" I asked.

"You do know how guilty that makes you sound," Eleanor said. "And you were in a hurry to leave your office as well."

"Which is why we wondered if there might be a personal involvement between you and Barlow," I added.

"The only contact I have with Officer Barlow is work-related."

I nodded. "It was my understanding that you were with Officer Barlow the entire time she was in the lounge?"

"I believe so, yes."

"So you're not certain?"

"I'm quite certain we were."

"Not even once?" Eleanor asked.

"Okay fine, she used the bathroom once. It's not like I went with her in there."

"And where is this bathroom located?"

"In the lounge."

"That's strange. Officer Yates told us it was in the hallway and that the one in the lounge is now used as a locker room."

Dr. Franks' eyes narrowed. "What does it matter?"

"It matters if you saw where Barlow disappeared to. It matters if you lost track of her completely," I said, taking a breath.

"Barlow used the bathroom, but wasn't out of my sight for more than five minutes."

"So where were you when she was in the

bathroom?"

"I was outside taking a smoke break."

"But there's no smoking on the prison grounds," Eleanor said.

"I'm perfectly aware of the rules, but the warden was off site and it's not like anyone cares."

"There are rules in place for a reason," I said.

"Yes, like the rules you broke that brought you here, you mean?" Franks said.

"We're not the ones suspected of murdering Lopez."

Dr. Franks shook his head. "Good luck proving that."

"That's a strange comment. All I know is that if you were out taking a smoke break you could have easily come to the warden's lounge and offed Lopez."

"Or Officer Barlow could have," Eleanor added.

"Look, I have no reason to want Lopez dead. And if either me or Barlow came back to the office area, why didn't either of you see us?"

"Who says we didn't?"

"You couldn't have because neither of us came back until after our lunch. Barlow was waiting for me in the hallway when I returned from my smoke."

"How did you get along with Lopez?"

"Fine enough, but she wasn't under my care."

"Why not?" Eleanor asked. "I thought that would be part of rehabilitation."

"Therapy doesn't agree with everyone. Lopez appeared to handle herself just fine. That's why she attained trustee status."

"How long was she a trustee?"

"I can't recall exactly. You'll have to speak with the warden about that."

"But we're asking you," I pressed.

"I'm sorry, but I don't know."

"Was Trudy your patient?"

"I really can't say. Patient confidentiality, you understand."

"Except that Trudy is dead."

"It doesn't matter whether she's dead."

"Are you aware of whether anyone was

harassing Trudy before her death?"

"I just told you that I can't tell you."

"So you can't tell us whether you heard the officers speak about it amongst themselves?"

"Officers aren't quite the gossipers you might think. It's frowned upon by the warden."

"That doesn't mean it doesn't happen."

"Barlow mentioned that the warden wasn't there the day Lopez was murdered," Eleanor said. "Where was she?"

Dr. Franks shook his head. "I'm sorry, but Felicia doesn't report to me."

"Felicia, eh?" Eleanor said. "Kind of familiar to be using the warden's first name."

Dr. Franks stood up. "Think what you want. I'm late for an appointment."

We stepped into the hallway when the doctor left and motioned Officer Miller inside.

"Would you like a cup of coffee?" I asked.

"Please, with sugar," Miller said as she sat down.

I fixed Miller's coffee and handed it to her. "I'm

sorry to hear you have to work overtime today."

"Only for an hour more. Officer Barlow decided to come in after all, which I'm happy about since I don't usually work the nightshift."

"I thought you only worked in quarantine."

"No, I work in D Pod most of the time."

"What's the difference between D Pod from F?"

"F Pod needs more supervision, for one. D Pod is minimum security."

"I see. Isn't Kelly Nash in D Pod?" I asked.

"Kelly Nash? Yes, I believe she was moved to D Pod a few months ago. How did her name come up?"

"We heard that she had to be separated from Trudy Taylor. We thought she might be someone we need to speak with."

"I know the warden has allowed you to question inmates and officers in relation to the murders of Trudy and now Lopez, but I'm quite sure she doesn't want you speaking to inmates from another pod who weren't even in F Pod when Trudy died."

"And how do you know what the warden is allowing us to do?"

"Because she told us there would be limits. I don't even know why I'm here. I rarely work in F Pod."

"I guessed as much, but I wanted to know what you've heard about Trudy Taylor. How did she get along with her fellow inmates?"

"Sorry, I can't help you."

"You must be aware of whether there were any problems," I pressed.

"I can't believe you had no clue why Kelly Nash was moved to D Pod," Eleanor said. "I believe there was a relationship of sorts between Kelly and Trudy."

"I don't have anything to say further on the matter," Miller said, standing up from the table.

"What's the policy for taking inmates to the bathroom at night?" I asked.

She froze. "They're escorted to the bathroom by an officer."

"And where is the officer supposed to be during

that bathroom run?"

"We don't have to be watching them go, you know."

"I understand that, but I expected a little more supervision. That's all we have to ask since you don't regularly work in F Pod."

"Were you working the day Lopez was murdered?" Eleanor asked.

"I was in D Pod the entire day."

I sighed when she left. It was quite apparent that interviewing Miller was a huge waste of time. I had no idea how long it was going to take to solve this case, but Eleanor and I couldn't stay here forever.

Chapter Thirteen

We walked back to our pod empty-handed investigation-wise, and I was so lost in thought that I almost didn't see Crusher barreling down on me. I stepped aside and we exchanged a glare that gave me chills. But I wasn't about to allow Crusher to intimidate me. And now I wondered if she was the one trying to scare me.

I waved Yolanda over and asked, "When did you say D Pod would be here for the volleyball game?"

"It was canceled. It seems the warden didn't think it was a good idea right now."

I was beyond miffed and complained to Officer Schulze. "Can you believe the warden canceled the volleyball game between us and D Pod?"

She smiled. "For some reason I don't see you

two as volleyball players."

"We're not, but we had hoped to question one of the women from D Pod —Kelly Nash," Eleanor said.

"I might be able to arrange something. Nash is in solitary, and I'm breaking the officer who works up there."

"But won't the cameras capture us going up there?"

"Yes, but you'll be delivering the meal trays." She winked.

Eleanor and I walked to the kitchen door and Schulze said, "Mason and Barton are taking the meal trays to solitary. So make it snappy and get them ready."

"I don't see why we have to do it," I grumbled. "My last trip to solitary wasn't a good one."

"You had better not let Schulze hear you or you'll be going there for a lengthy stay," Teresa said. "On the other hand, maybe you should stay there because Crusher is gunning for you, Barton."

"About what this time?"

"You didn't think she was going to let the cornbread thing go, did you?"

"But that wasn't my fault."

"Crusher doesn't understand or care whose fault it is. All she understands is crushing." Teresa laughed, slapping her fist into an open hand.

I was rattled, but had to stay on task as we pushed the tray cart to solitary. We had no longer followed Officer Schulze in when we heard inmates making a ruckus.

"Calm down," Schulze shouted. "Your chow is here."

She nodded at us and we began handing trays through the slots as they were opened by Schulze. But at the last door, the mesh window was open. I stared at an inmate with long dark hair and pretty blue eyes.

"Are you Kelly Nash?" I asked.

"Yes, who are you?"

"I'm here to ask you a few questions about Trudy. We're trying to find out who murdered her."

Tears began coursing down Kelly's face. "I hope you can. I only wish I hadn't been forced to leave F Pod. It's my fault she was murdered."

"Why do you think that?" I asked.

"Well, my involvement with Trudy for one. I think that cellmate of hers was jealous about my relationship with Trudy and told the warden, because I was moved not long after I had an altercation with Lopez."

"So Lopez snitched on you?"

"I'm pretty sure, but I can't prove it."

"How long was Lopez a trustee?"

"Just a few weeks before I was moved to D Pod."

"But don't the inmates frown on snitches?" Eleanor asked.

"Yes, but it was hard to prove who told the warden. Some of the inmates think an officer was responsible, but Trudy never had any problems with the officers before. She was a beautician, and styled the officers' hair, too."

"And her fellow inmates?"

"They idolized her. You'd be shocked how she

transformed how many of them looked. That's why I heard they were talking riot. Well, that and because the warden wasn't moving on the investigation. I'm not sure why she allowed you two on the case, but I hope you find out who murdered Trudy. I'd be careful with Lopez, though, she has the warden's ear."

"Not anymore; she's dead."

"Now that's poetic justice."

"If Lopez had you moved, I wonder why she would murder Trudy?" I mused.

"Maybe Lopez made a move on Trudy and she rejected her," Eleanor suggested. "And she murdered Trudy so nobody would find out."

"That sounds like Lopez. She's a control freak and she wouldn't like it if anyone found out she was sweet on another inmate," Kelly said. "Unless someone found out she had snitched," Kelly added. "I would have made sure the inmates knew it if I wasn't removed from F Pod." She sighed. "Perhaps if I had the chance, Trudy wouldn't be dead now."

"Don't blame yourself for that," Eleanor said

sympathetically.

I paused for a moment before I finally said, "Thank you, Kelly. You've given us something to think about. We don't have much more time."

"That's all we have here," Kelly said, "time."

Eleanor and I stepped away from Kelly's door. We nodded at Officer Schulze for allowing us to speak with Kelly.

I pushed the cart as we made way for the kitchen, but Barlow blocked my path in the hallway.

Her eyes narrowed. "Where were you?"

"Can you move please? I have to push the cart back to the kitchen so they know we passed the trays."

"What trays?" Barlow asked, stepping toward me.

"If you're trying to intimidate me, it's not working."

"I'm writing you a ticket for that," Barlow said as she took a pen and pad from her pocket.

"Save it, Barlow," Schulze said. "They were

helping me pass trays in solitary."

Barlow's mouth fell open and she then snapped it closed. "I see. Well, you could have told me."

"I wasn't aware you were here yet."

I watched Officer Barlow move through the door that led to the offices. I thought she was headed straight for the warden, but I gave up caring. I was getting sick of her bullying.

"That woman doesn't have a decent bone in her body," Eleanor sneered.

"Be careful. You can't speak about an officer like that. Those tickets can add up, and it won't look good at your parole hearing," Schultz said.

I wished I could tell Schulze who we really were. She was the only decent uniformed officer.

Eleanor and I walked to the kitchen and moved the cart against the wall. I noticed Jana leaned against the opposite wall, sweat rolling off her face, her hair hanging in drenched ringlets.

I rushed over to her and asked, "Are you okay?"

She stared at me. "I'm fine."

"She's withdrawing," Teresa said. For once she

looked genuinely concerned.

"Oh, because of Mary's missing shipment?"

"What do you know about that?"

"I just heard something," I said.

"Well, un-hear it," Teresa cautioned me. "It's better for you health."

I merely nodded. "What can we do for Jana?"

"She'll have to tough it out."

"But she needs medical help. Someone should call the doctor."

"You just don't get it. You have no idea how hard it is to even see the doctor. And the warden will have this place turned upside down."

I sighed. "But she needs to be in her cell, not here."

"I agree. Why don't you help her? I can't leave the kitchen"

I nodded and put an arm around Jana and helped her to her cell. Officer Schulze rushed over. "What happened?"

"Jana's sick."

Once we were in Jana's cell Schulze lifted Jana's

chin slightly. "I thought you knew better than to mess with drugs, Jana," she said with a shake of her head. "She needs to be seen by the doctor immediately."

"But I can't," Jana said.

"You don't have a choice, and neither do I. I have to report this, and you know it," Schulze said as she left.

"Mary is going to kill me," Jana whispered. "This is all my fault. I shouldn't have been taking that oxy, but how was I to know that Mary wouldn't be able to get her stuff."

I sat on Jana's bed. "But don't you see the dangers of that?"

"I do when I feel like this. I was going through a rough time. My mother had died and I couldn't go to the funeral."

"That is tough, but I know you can beat this. When you do, you'll feel much better about everything."

The warden and an army of officers hurried into the pod. Barlow glared at me as she took in the scene. "Did you give this inmate the drugs, Barton?" Officer Barlow demanded.

I stood up and faced her. "Me? I haven't even been here long enough to build up a drug business yet."

"That's not funny, Agnes," Eleanor whispered.

We left the cell and an announcement came over the public address system: "Line up outside your cells for the check."

We raced to our cell to find two officers we'd never seen before tossing items out of our drawers and cabinet. They then overturned our mattresses.

Officer Barlow moved to enter our cell and I protested, "I don't want her to check our cell."

The warden came over. "What's the problem here?"

"These officers have already checked our cell. There's no need for Officer Barlow to check it."

"Is that because you have contraband?" Barlow asked.

"No, it's because you might add some contraband just so we get a charge or sent to solitary."

"That's a serious allegation," Warden Geyer said.

"Since you've already been to solitary today, I didn't think you would mind going back," Barlow said.

"We were only handing out the food trays," I exclaimed.

"I sense some animosity here," Warden Geyer said. "I hope you're not on a personal vendetta against Barton and Mason for questioning you yesterday."

"Of course not!"

"Please help with the search in the other cells."

Barlow stalked into our cell anyway. She wiped her hand over a metal shelf and returned with a banana. "What do we have here? Planning on making a little hooch?"

"You must have planted that!" I exclaimed.

Eleanor shuffled her feet. "I might have brought that back from breakfast." When I narrowed my eyes at her she exclaimed, "But I get hungry at night!"

"That's what commissary items are for," Geyer said.

"Everyone knows you can't make hooch with bananas," said Mel from a neighboring cell. "Bananas have potassium. It has to be an acid-based fruit. Google it if you don't believe me."

"Yeah, Google it," Eleanor added as she puffed up her chest. "I knew it the whole time."

"You can't be serious. She wants us to Google it," Barlow choked out.

"I think that would be a good job for you," Warden Geyer said. "Let me know what you find out." She turned to us, "Don't take any more food from the chow hall. And you are to show Officer Barlow the respect she is due or you'll find yourself in solitary."

I nodded curtly at the warden, but focused my attention across the pod at the inmate I had seen the night before in the bathroom. At least I knew where to go next. I had a few questions for her.

The officers ended their search, and Eleanor

and I cleaned up the mess that was left behind. I frowned to find my shampoo bottle cracked and spilled on the floor. I'd need another trip to the commissary after we questioned the inmates who were still on our list.

Eleanor and I missed lunch because we were distributing trays in solitary. Office Schulze said loud enough for everyone to hear, "Until further notice, your yard privileges are suspended."

"What?" the inmates called out. "Why?"

Warden Geyer sighed. "Until we find out how drugs are getting into the prison, there will be no yard time. And your time in the commons area will be limited to an hour after lunch."

I swallowed hard. "This can't be good," I said.

"I think there's going to be trouble, and soon." Eleanor sighed.

Angry inmates congregated in the commons area. "What are we going to do, Mary?" one of her cronies, Frankie, asked.

"How should I know? We'll have to bide our time. I better not find out who snitched to the warden."

"Yes, and we all know who's chummy with the warden, now, don't we," Crusher said, rubbing her fist with her other hand.

I wanted to tell Mary it was all her fault for giving Jana the drugs. "I'm sure it must be a routine sweep is all," I said. "I'm certain they happen frequently."

"Except that we've never lost our yard time for a spot check before," Mary said.

Chapter Fourteen

We didn't stick around, not when the inmates were riled. I moved to where I spotted the inmate I saw the night before. I knocked on the cell door and asked, "Can I speak with you?"

"About?" the inmate asked.

"I wanted to ask you a few questions about the bathroom visit last night. We've been trying to find out who murdered Trudy."

"Come in before Mary sees you. I don't need her thinking I'm part of your narc squad."

Eleanor and I hurried inside. "I won't bother you with any denials since that's not what I have to say. Is it normal for the officers to escort more than one inmate to the bathroom at night?"

"Not normal, but it happens."

"What do you know about the day Trudy died?"

"I hope you don't expect me to know if she used the bathroom that night."

"Is it possible that two inmates were taken to the bathroom and that's how Trudy was murdered?"

"But I thought I heard you say to the other inmates that you weren't convinced an officer didn't do it."

"We still have to look at both sides. So if an inmate didn't do it, would a guard have the time to kill an inmate?"

"Why not?"

"But the other officer would have to be detained if the guard killed Trudy," Eleanor said, "and they'd have to be unaware of the other officer taking Trudy."

"I'm sure you could figure this out without me," the inmate said. "I'd appreciate it if you left my name out of it."

"Of course. I don't even know your name, nor will I ask you what it is."

"One last question," Eleanor began, "do the

officers always stay outside the bathroom when the inmates are in there at night."

"Your friend saw that for herself last night."

I nodded in agreement. "Where can we find a Shelly Rhodes?"

"Go up the stairs, first cell on the left. You can't miss her. Shelly doesn't have eyebrows."

We crossed the commons area and climbed the stairs. We were panting hard by the time we reached the second tier of cells.

"Is this Shelly's Rhodes's cell?" I called out.

"Who's asking?" a tattooed woman asked from her bunk.

"I just had a few questions to ask her."

"Come inside then."

"We're trying to figure out who murdered Trudy Taylor."

"I think we all know that."

"It was my understanding you and Trudy didn't get along. Love triangle perhaps," I suggested.

The inmate jumped up and was in my face. "I'm not like that. Trudy fried my hair when she permed it. It still hasn't grown back yet."

I willed myself not to stare at her eyebrow-less brow. "I see. Well, that's hardly a reason to want the woman dead."

"I might have jumped her, but she was alive when I left her cell."

"When did that happen?"

"The afternoon before she was murdered."

Her cellmate sat up. "I can vouch for Shelly. She never left this cell that night, and reported to the kitchen that morning. She had kitchen duty."

"And your name is?"

"Macy Jalene, but if the warden comes around asking me questions, we'll know for sure you're a snitch."

"Agnes is not a snitch. She's been my best friend for years and hasn't let me down yet," Eleanor insisted.

Eleanor and I went back down the stairs, but Mary's muscle, Frankie and Midge, barred our way.

"Could you please move?" I asked sweetly.

"Why, are you planning to speak with the

warden about Mary again?" Frankie asked.

"I'd never do that. I don't even know that much about her drug peddling."

"You're going to get us killed, Agnes," Eleanor whispered.

"Well, I won't be speaking to the warden again. I only did that so I could question the officers. And we've already questioned them about Trudy's murder."

Laura pushed her way through. "These two are most likely suffering from dementia. I doubt they remember their names in the morning," she sneered.

"And I thought you were nice when we were in quarantine."

"Looks can be deceiving." Frankie laughed.

They moved aside. We had to question the last inmate on our list soon.

I found Yolanda and Velma with Char, who was picking her teeth with a toothpick. "Oh look, your snitch friends are here," Char said.

"We're not snitches," I swore.

"That's not what everyone thinks. Mary thinks that's why the spot check happened today," Char said.

"I wish everyone would quit saying that. I can't help but notice, Char, that you claim all us first-timers are cops or snitches. What have either of us done that would make you think that?"

Char was in my face now. "You're too chummy with the warden, for one. Why would she allow you to question the officers like that?"

"Does it matter? Or don't you care whether they find out who murdered Trudy?"

"And whoever did it also killed Lopez," Yolanda said.

"Exactly, but for the life of me I can't understand who would be able to get into the offices to kill her. I mean, if an inmate was responsible, how would she get in there? We were the only ones, and all the officers have alibis."

"You can't take them at their word," Char sneered. "They'd lie in a second, and they stick up for one another."

"I understand how you feel, but we're doing all we can."

"Where can we find Fran Wilson?" Eleanor asked. "She's the last person on our list."

"Figure it out yourself," Char snarled as she strode away.

I sighed. "I shouldn't have spoken to her like that," I mused.

"No, but luckily for the moment she hasn't decided to knock your teeth out," Velma said. "Of course I can't say the same for Crusher. Please be careful, ladies."

"Check out that cell over there," Yolanda said.

Yolanda and Velma left, leaving us alone. I didn't like the atmosphere. From the glances thrown our way from the inmates, all of them thought we were snitches.

Eleanor and I went to the cell Yolanda indicated and found an older woman sitting on her bunk doing a crossword puzzle. "I wondered how long it was going to take for you ladies to come visit me."

"Why haven't we seen you out and about?"

"I stay in my cell most of the time. I injured my back sometime ago."

"How?" Eleanor asked.

"Do I really have to tell you?" she asked. "We all know who really runs this place, and it's not the warden. This pod has its own rules, and Mary is the chief. Don't forget that. If you cross Mary, you're done."

"I believe you, but what do you know about Trudy's death?"

"Enough to know it was murder."

"Do you think Mary killed her?"

"You tell me."

"Well, if all the inmates are locked up, who was the officer that night?"

When Fran didn't say anything, Eleanor sighed. "We have to know," Eleanor said. "We were told that Officer Barlow doesn't work nights."

"No," she finally said. "But Officer Barlow showed up early."

"Thank you so much. We'll never mention your

name to anyone."

"That's a promise I expect you to keep."

We left Fran's cell and I shook my head. "I guess that's it then. We'll never find out who murdered Trudy and Lopez," I said loud enough for everyone to hear.

Eleanor threw up her arms. "I give up!"

I then lowered my voice. "Eleanor, let's head to the bathroom. I have to pee."

Luckily none of the inmates blocked our path to the bathroom. I was beginning to feel quite on edge, but hoped we'd be able to snow them.

We had no sooner entered the bathroom when Mary's muscle, Frankie and Midge, shoved us further into the room. Mary surfaced from a stall, and her hands slipped to her hips.

"You know my grandmother is from Alabama, born and raised. She taught me how to be a proper southern lady and to always respect my elders. But the both of you are pushing all the wrong buttons. The only good snitch is a dead one."

"But we're not ... ."

"Save it. Barlow gave us the scoop."

"Officer Barlow?"

"Yes, she's been most helpful."

"Meaning she's sneaking drugs into the prison for you?"

"That's quite an assumption. Are you sure there's nothing else you plan to say to me." Mary brushed her fingernails against her shirt. "I've been known to be understanding."

Laura rushed into the bathroom and Mary nodded at her as she joined the group of thugs. "Sorry I'm late." While she frowned as if she uncertain, Laura continued to stand with Mary.

"If you didn't want the powers-that-be knowing about your drug business, you shouldn't have hooked so many of the inmates on that stuff. Jana is in withdrawal because of you, and an officer had no other choice than to report it to the warden."

"See, we didn't snitch," Eleanor added. "It was your doing, Mary."

"Let me at Barton," Crusher said from the opposite side of the bathroom, clenching and unclenching her fists.

"Not yet," I choked out. "You need to know the kind of person Mary really is."

"You remind me of Trudy a little. A do-gooder to the end, or so I heard," Mary coolly said.

Officer Schulze hurried into the bathroom. "What's going on in here?"

"Nothing," I said. "We're just talking."

"Hands off, Mary! I'm certain you wouldn't care for a stay in solitary," Schulze threatened.

Mary glanced at her fingernails. "I never put my hands on anyone. You should know that."

"All of you, out," Schulze commanded.

They were all ushered into the common area and Schulze ordered everyone to their cells. Inmates filed from the room to comply, but I never even had a chance.

Chapter Fifteen

Crusher came barreling at me. I brought up my hand as if I were going to karate chop her, and I kicked my leg up.

Crusher was almost on me, but ... she tripped over my foot. She sailed through the air and landed face first into one of the seats bolted to the floor.

"Ouch!" Eleanor muttered.

When she didn't move, I shrieked, "I think I knocked her unconscious! Crusher needs help!"

Inmates raced back into the commons area. Officer Schulze shouted for help into the intercom on the wall. Inmates and officers alike flooded the area. Schulze handcuffed me, and Laura asked, "You did this to Crusher?"

"Yes! I just couldn't take it any longer," I shouted as officers dragged me from the room to solitary.

I pounded the metal door and winced as my hand began to throb. I had gone and done it now. I had inadvertently knocked out Crusher. I wouldn't allow myself to feel good about that, although it did make me smile. While she might have sustained a serious injury, I could have been crushed for real.

I felt I had the case figured out, but how will I be able to tell the warden now? When Mary mentioned Barlow telling her I snitched, I knew how Trudy died.

I huddled on the thin mattress pad and rubbed my arms. Would I face an assault charge now?

The sound of the key in the lock startled me and I stood up. The warden motioned me out of the cell. "Keep quiet. I'll take you through the back way."

I allowed myself to be led down the series of hallways until we came to the offices. When I walked into the warden's office, Deputy Director Smith was standing. Eleanor, Mary, and Officers

Barlow and Schulze were there, too. Mary was handcuffed.

"Are you okay?" Eleanor blubbered.

"Yes, but why are we all here?"

Warden Geyer walked behind her desk and took a seat. "Barton, what have you found out in regards to the deaths of Trudy Taylor and Maria Lopez?"

"I can't say on the grounds that I'll be brutally murdered," I said as I warily glanced at Mary.

"Don't worry about that now. Mary is heading to the Women's Huron Valley Corrections Facility when we're done here."

"You can't do that!" Mary screeched.

"I can and I am. You'll be facing drug charges to add on to your original sentence. Another thirty years from the sounds of the judge I spoke with."

Mary gnashed her teeth. "I'll get you, Barton!"

Warden Geyer shook her head. "It wasn't her. I found out how the drugs were coming into the prison. Your reign of terror is over."

I smiled. "You might have to add to her

sentence, but I'm reluctant to tell you the particulars now."

"You're free to talk, I assure you," Deputy Director Smith said.

"Mary just about confessed that she killed Trudy."

"I did not!"

"Trudy was tired of your drug peddling, and that's why you killed her."

"Mary doesn't have the guts," Eleanor said. "All she's good at is dishing out the orders."

"That's true," I said turning to face Barlow. "You're the one who killed Maria Lopez."

"How do you figure that? I have an airtight alibi. You said so yourself."

"Yes, until I found out you and Mary are in cahoots. She told us how you lied and told her we were snitches. We haven't snitched on anyone!"

"If you'd tell an inmate like Mary that we were snitches, you're capable of murdering Lopez," Eleanor shouted.

"Do I have to stand here and listen to this,

warden?"

"Yes, I think you do. I thought you knew better than to bring drugs into this prison."

"That's not true! I don't want to be on their side of the fence," Barlow scoffed.

"Face it," I said, "you're caught, Barlow!"

"What possible proof do you have?"

The warden pulled out a bag of white powder. "I found this in your locker."

Barlow's eyes bulged slightly. "Why would you go into my locker?"

"I brought in a drug-sniffing canine. I wanted to assure myself that none of my officers were part of the drug trafficking. Schulze, cuff Barlow."

Barlow's face reddened. "Please, I didn't have anything to do with this. I never told Mary that Barton and Mason were snitches. This is a set-up!"

"I already told the warden that," Mary said. "I had no reason to kill Trudy, although I can imagine why they would think that I had."

"Yes, you hate snitches," Eleanor said. "For someone like you, that's all the reason you need."

"There's never a good reason to murder anyone," I insisted.

Police officers filed into the room, taking Officer Barlow into custody. There was something about the look in her eye that gave me pause, but I quickly shook it off.

"Take Mary to solitary," Warden Geyer said. "It will be better if we pack up her things. I don't want any further problems with the other inmates about her departure."

"But what will you do with the other inmates who follow her?" I asked.

"We'll be sending both Frankie and Midge to different pods. That will help for a start."

"How is Crusher doing?"

"You knocked her out cold."

"No, she tripped. I'd like to see her if I can."

"Why? I hope you know she wanted you dead."

"Or seriously injured," Eleanor chimed in.

"Did you even check the cameras near your lounge?" I asked the warden. "You told us you'd get back to us about it."

"I did. I tried to check the recordings, but apparently the cameras weren't functional. Officer Barlow must have disabled them."

I gave Eleanor a sidelong look. "What about the broken lock on the storeroom door?"

"It wasn't broken, just like I told you. I have no idea why Officer Yates told you otherwise."

"Thanks for allowing us to investigate," I said.

"But what about Laura Keelie?" Eleanor asked. "She was part of Mary's group."

"I don't think she was all that involved. She came here when you did."

"Good job, warden," Smith said. "I wasn't sure you were ready for a promotion, but I'll promote you when I secure the director position. I can't see anyone else getting the deputy director job now. There aren't any wardens I know who have broken up a drug ring like this in their prisons."

"I appreciate that, Smith, but it was bad enough that drugs found their way into my prison to begin with."

"It's a constant battle, but we're on the winning

team this time," Smith patted Warden Geyer on the back.

"Where are we going now?" I asked.

"Back to F Pod where you belong," Geyer said. "I'll bet none of the inmates will give you any problems now that you knocked Crusher out." She laughed.

"Can't I see her before we go back. I feel awful about what happened."

"It can wait until tomorrow. Crusher isn't in a position to talk right now."

I sighed. For some reason I felt it was important to speak with her, but I didn't have a choice.

Officer Schulze walked us back, and I rushed to the storeroom door, rattling the handle until it opened. "It looks like the lock is broken after all."

"Leave it alone, Barton," Schulze said.

"If you say so." I'd let it go all right — for now.

Eleanor and I hurried into the pod. The inmates were locked in their cells. I sat on my bunk facing Eleanor. I waited until Schulze locked us in and left before I said, "I'm not sure about Officer Barlow's guilt now."

"What are you talking about?" Eleanor asked. "Barlow worked the day Trudy was murdered."

"I know, but that doesn't mean an inmate didn't kill Trudy."

"How?"

"A guard could have taken an inmate out and become distracted."

"So you think two of them were out of their cells?"

"I don't know. I'm wondering how Barlow had the time to kill Lopez. We knew where she was most of the time."

"They found drugs in her locker, didn't you hear?"

"Yes, but they could have been planted while she was busy or any time she was working," I suggested. "Besides, we know how the drugs were coming in, with the dirty laundry, remember?"

"So where does that leave us?"

"Why would the warden tell us the lock on the storeroom door wasn't broken when it clearly is?"

"She also claims the cameras near the warden's lounge weren't functional," Eleanor said.

"Meaning anyone could have murdered Lopez. But why would they kill her?"

"We're right back at the beginning. Why was Trudy really murdered?"

"She knew something that Lopez didn't want to get out," I insisted.

"So you think Lopez killed Trudy?"

"Yes. She might have shared something with Trudy that she feared would get out."

"And whoever killed Lopez worried that she'd talk?" Eleanor asked.

"Exactly. We'll have to wait until tomorrow before we can check out a few things."

"Like what?"

"We have to make sure we're the ones taking in the dirty laundry tomorrow."

"To see if drugs are still coming in that way?" Eleanor asked.

"Yes, and I have a feeling they will be."

I pulled the blanket over me. I didn't know who

besides a guard would be able to help Lopez, but I had a feeling tomorrow we'd find out — or so I hoped. We'd been in here too long as it was.

Chapter Sixteen

"Hello, girls," Char said as we walked to the only available table in the chow hall.

Yolanda and Velma were all smiles. "You're the most admired inmate in Westbrook, Agnes," Yolanda said.

"Why is that?" I asked.

"You took down Crusher?"

"That wasn't like it ... ." Eleanor kicked me under the table, and I said, "She had it coming!"

I glanced around the hall. "Where is Mary and her clan?"

"I heard Mary was rushed out of here this morning," Velma said, "along with Frankie and Midge."

"How would you know that for sure?" I asked.

"Well, they're not here now and officers packed

up their belongings. That's a sure sign that they're gone for good."

"I told you that Laura was a cop," Char said. "Kind of funny that Mary was taken down not long after she showed up."

"Something like that takes months to organize," I insisted.

"We heard Officer Barlow had drugs in her locker," Eleanor said with a shrug.

"No way would Barlow do something like that," Char hissed. "I tell you it had to be that Laura. She's gone too."

"She is?" I asked. "Now that is strange. Perhaps you're right."

Eleanor and I were on our feet when the work assignment announcement came on. Officer Schulze simply nodded at us as we approached.

"Can we work in receiving today?" I asked.

"Why?"

"We need the fresh air because yard time was taken away."

"I believe it will be reinstated today."

"Please," I implored.

"Not unless you tell me why you really want to do that job."

I was hesitant. Could I trust Schulze? "I'm not sure Barlow is guilty of bringing drugs into the prison. It comes in with the laundry."

Schulze's hands moved to her hips. "And what makes you think that?"

"We overheard Mary talking outside with a man when we were on trash detail. We couldn't see his face, though."

"Fine, but I'll have to speak with the warden about this. She won't be happy."

I sighed. "I'd hate to see Barlow going to jail for something she didn't do."

"But you thought she killed Lopez."

"I know that, but I feel Barlow was set up."

"It doesn't matter," Warden Geyer said, walked up to us. "Bring them to my office."

I swallowed hard and felt absolute dread at what was about to happen. "She did it," I mouthed to Eleanor.

I opened my eyes as wide as I could as we passed Deputy Director Smith, but he was too busy reading through a file. I wanted to call out about who really orchestrated the murder of Trudy and then Lopez, but who would believe me?

The warden's office door slammed closed behind us. The warden then sauntered behind her desk and took a seat. "I see you doubt my word."

"No, I doubt Officer Barlow brought drugs into this prison."

"Well, how else would they get in her locker?"

"You put them there," I said.

The warden was no longer smiling. "That's absurd. Why would I do that?"

"So nobody would find out that you ordered Lopez to kill Trudy Taylor," Eleanor said.

"And I did that because?"

"Because Lopez mentioned that Trudy was planning to tell Mary about your plot to end her business and ship her out of here."

"Would that be such a bad thing?"

"It would if you decided to frame an officer," I

said.

"I believe Trudy found out that you were planning to use Mary to look good enough for that promotion you wanted. She was going to make it known, and you told Lopez to murder Trudy."

"How would she do that during lockup?"

"At first I thought an officer was responsible, but now I know Lopez killed Trudy in their cell and you helped her move the body to the bathroom."

The warden's eyes bulged. "I would never do anything like that to get a promotion. I wanted the drug flow stopped, but I never ordered Lopez to kill anyone."

"I think you killed Lopez," Eleanor exclaimed. "We all know Officer Barlow was elsewhere when that happened."

"That lock to the storeroom is broken," I began, "and you were supposed to be out of the prison, but then you appeared when the the body was found."

"You're both crazy!"

"Did Lopez threaten to tell someone?" I

pressed.

The warden eased back in her chair. “It doesn’t matter now that you won’t be here long enough to tell any more stories. I had already planned to have you relocated to Huron Valley.”

Eleanor sucked in a breath. “So you’re admitting that you ordered Lopez to kill Trudy, and then you killed Lopez to cover it up?” She laughed hysterically.

“What’s wrong with your friend?” Warden Geyer said.

“Insanity plea?”

“It doesn’t matter. None of it matters. So what if I told Lopez to murder Trudy? It was her fault for telling Trudy my plans to begin with. But Lopez had to feel guilty about it, and I knew before long she’d tell the deputy director. I had no choice. I had to kill her. I couldn’t trust anyone else to do the job.”

“Then all you had to do was frame Officer Barlow. You probably made sure she came in early that day.”

"Well, I had to come up with some way the drugs were coming in. It's plausible that Barlow was covering her tracks by murdering both Trudy and Lopez. She's not well liked."

There was a knock at the door and Deputy Director Smith and U.S. Marshal Cain strode into the room.

"What is this about?" Geyer asked as she shakily stood.

"I want to thank you ladies for your help," Cain said. "It took some convincing before I was able to persuade the deputy director to go along with your investigation and wiretap the warden's office."

"How could you, Smith?" Warden Geyer said near tears.

"How could you Felicia? I've heard of some pretty far-fetched plots to get a promotion, but this was so unnecessary. You've been my first pick to replace me, but now you'll be going to prison."

"I-It wasn't me. I was set up, I tell you."

"No, you set up Officer Barlow," I said. "The drugs are coming in with the dirty laundry," I informed Smith.

"Schulze told me and the truck is being gone through as we speak." His brow furrowed. "I was shocked when the marshal told me you two were undercover inmates. Women your age should be... ."

"I know. We're supposed to be sitting on a rocking chair, knitting," I interjected. "Does that mean we can get out of here today."

"Your husbands are waiting for you outside. They've been camped out in the parking lot the last few days," Smith said.

There was another knock on the door, and as Cain opened it one of Mary's cronies, Laura Keelie stood there! Why was she here?

She stepped into the office and then closed the door. "Things have certainly gotten out of hand. When I was assigned to investigate the drug smuggling in the prison, I had no idea that someone was assigned to investigate the death of Trudy Taylor." She took a breath. "Well, while I didn't learn much of anything, you ladies found out plenty. I'm glad that you weren't killed by Crusher."

"And I'm glad that Char didn't catch up to you before you left the prison population. She had you pegged for a cop the whole time."

"But how?"

"You shouldn't have acted quite so mousy in quarantine and suddenly pop out of your shell so quickly."

"I suppose you're right, but I didn't think anyone would notice the change."

"Except that Char is a regular. She doesn't trust anyone."

Epilogue

We walked with a smiling Officer Schulze to our cell. "I should have known you ladies had more of a interest in Trudy's murder than you should have. If the inmates had wanted to riot, they would have when Trudy died. I must admit that you're good investigators."

"Yes, but we've been doing that for years back home in Tawas," I informed her.

I packed my belongings and stared at the candy bars and bags of chips that I hadn't eaten. I then poked my head out of my cell and asked, "Does anyone want our candy and chips?"

Char was the first through the door, followed by Yolanda and Velma.

Char looked down at our packed bags. "Cops, just like I knew the whole time."

"Aren't we a little old to be cops?" I asked.

She shrugged and made off with the Snickers.

"Will we ever know who you really are?" Yolanda asked.

"We're simply undercover inmates." I winked.

Eleanor gave Yolanda and Velma a quick hug. "I'm sure going to miss you girls. Thank you for being so kind to us."

"Yes, I don't think we'd have been able to do it without either of you, and Char. I wish we had time to say a proper goodbye," I said.

"Char would never admit that she likes both of you. It's just not who she is," Yolanda explained. She then moved in. "Is it true what they say about the warden? That she was responsible for the deaths of Trudy and Lopez?"

"And she set up Officer Barlow by putting drugs in her locker," Eleanor added.

"Actually, the warden ordered Lopez to murder Trudy," I began, "She was the one who murdered Lopez."

"Wow, I had no idea the warden was so

twisted," Yolanda said.

"I wonder which prison she's going to?" Velma asked.

"I'm not sure, but Huron Valley sure would be cozy — she sent Mary there," I said with a shrug.

"Really, so Mary is gone for good?" Velma asked. "I'm not sorry to see her leave."

I swiped at the tears that appeared. Schulze cleared her throat. "That's our cue to leave. Tell everyone I said goodbye."

"I will," Yolanda said as she sniffled.

"There are never long goodbyes here," Schulze explained. "Somehow I knew word has been leaked to the inmates, but they deserve to know who was responsible for Trudy's death. After all, that's why you came here."

"Yes, and I'm shocked we made it through. I think I'll carry my memories of this place for a long time."

"Who are you kidding?" Eleanor laughed. "You'll forget by tomorrow. She forgets gals our age have trouble with our short-term memory."

My Andrew was waiting for us when we went back to the offices. He didn't say a word; he didn't have to, but he did enclose me in quite a hug. I gasped. "I can't breathe."

"That will teach you to leave me for so long."

"Where is Mr. Wilson?" Eleanor asked, searching the hallway.

"Here he comes," I pointed out.

Mr. Wilson shook his head as he pushed his walker along. "You'd think a place like this would at least have a handicapped bathroom."

"Oh, Mr. Wilson. Come here and give me a big sloppy kiss," Eleanor exclaimed.

I averted my eyes when they embraced and pointed out the hospital wing. "I have to say goodbye to someone," I told Andrew and he merely nodded. That's part of the reason I love Andrew. He knows when I need time to myself.

I spotted Dr. Wright and smiled. "Can I see Crusher? I won't be but a moment, I promise. Eleanor and I are leaving."

"I heard. She's in the last bed."

"How is she?"

"Just a little concussion. She's had worse."

I crossed the room and peeked behind the curtain and waved at Crusher. "Is it okay if I speak with you for a moment?"

"Go ahead. It's not like I'm going anywhere soon. That doctor insists I stay here a few days."

I walked to her bedside. "I'm really sorry about what happened. I never meant to hurt you."

She cocked one brow. "You do know I wanted to kill you, right?"

"Yes, but that doesn't mean I wanted to see you hurt."

"No problem. I'll just tell the other inmates I took a dive so they think you're invincible. Especially since everyone called you a snitch."

"Thanks to Mary."

"I heard all about everything that happened. You're both pretty gutsy going undercover in a place like this."

"Or stupid," I replied.

Smith was waiting for me when I walked back

into the lobby. "I wish I could have spoken to Officer Barlow before we left. She might not even want to come back after what happened."

"She'll be back, especially when she finds out she'll be the deputy warden when she returns."

"I had wondered why there wasn't one."

"We've been reviewing the officers to make the right decision. I believe she's the right person for the job. Good luck ladies," Smith smiled as he walked away.

I rejoined Andrew and he smiled as we stood in the entranceway of Westbrook Prison. Mr. Wilson and Eleanor followed us as we stepped outside, the sunshine nearly blinding me. I had forgotten how much I had missed while Eleanor and I were undercover. We were fortunate that we had our freedom with our loving husbands at our side.

About The Author

Madison's writing journey began at the age of 44 and it wasn't until four years later that she wrote the book that she thought had the most potential, one that readers would really enjoy. A series that takes place in the real town of Tawas, Michigan, one of Madison's favorite vacation spot as a child.

Although sleep-deprived from working third shift, she knew if she used what she had learned while caring for senior citizens to good use, it would result in something quite unique. The Agnes Barton Senior Sleuths Mystery Series has forever changed Madison's life, and propelled her onto the USA Today Bestsellers list.

She now works full time as a writer from home where she continues to write cozy mysteries and historical romances as Clara Kincaid. Visit Madison on the web at: http://www.MadisonJohns.com. Sign up for Madison's mystery newsletter list at: http://eepurl.com/4kFsH.

Other Books by Madison Johns

An Agnes Barton Senior Sleuths Mystery Series

Armed and Outrageous
Grannies, Guns & Ghosts
Senior Snoops
Trouble in Tawas
Treasure in Tawas
Bigfoot in Tawas
High Seas Honeymoon
Outrageous Vegas Vacation
Birds of a Feather

An Agnes Barton Paranormal Mystery Series

Haunted Hijinks
Ghostly Hijinks
Spooky Hijinks
Hair-Raising Hijinks

An Agnes Barton Holiday Mystery

The Great Turkey Caper
The Great Christmas Caper

Kimberly Steele Sweet Romance

Pretty and Pregnant
Pretty and Pregnant Again

An Agnes Barton/Kimberly Steele Romance

Pretty, Hip & Dead

A Cajun Cooking Mystery

Target of Death

Lake Forest Witches

Meows, Magic & Murder
Meows, Magic & Manslaughter
Meows, Magic & Missing

A Pet Recovery Center Mystery

Up the Creek Without a Poodle

Kelly Gray Sweet Romance

Redneck Romance

Paranormal Romance

Clan of the Werebear, the Complete Series

Shadow Creek Shifters

Katlyn
Taken
Tessa

Western Historical Romance
Writing as Clara Kincaid
Nevada Brides Series

McKenna
Cadence
Kayla
Abigail
Penelope

Johanna, Bride of Michigan, is 26th in the unprecedented 50-book, **American Mail-Order Brides** series
Johanna: Bride of Michigan

CPSIA information can be obtained
at www.ICGtesting.com
Printed in the USA
LVOW10s2134160717
541558LV00011BA/657/P